THE HAUNTING
OF WILDWOOD PLANTATION

STEPHANIE MCMAHAN

THE HAUNTING OF WILDWOOD PLANTATION

iUniverse books may be ordered through booksellers or by contacting:

iUniverse
1663 Liberty Drive
Bloomington, IN 47403
www.iuniverse.com
844-349-9409

Because of the dynamic nature of the Internet, any web addresses or links contained in this book may have changed since publication and may no longer be valid. The views expressed in this work are solely those of the author and do not necessarily reflect the views of the publisher, and the publisher hereby disclaims any responsibility for them.

Any people depicted in stock imagery provided by Getty Images are models, and such images are being used for illustrative purposes only. Certain stock imagery © Getty Images.

ISBN: 978-1-6632-4709-4 (sc)
ISBN: 978-1-6632-4710-0 (e)

Library of Congress Control Number: 2022919810

Print information available on the last page.

iUniverse rev. date: 11/14/2022

To my students at Barre City Elementary and Middle School,
who inspired me with their curiosity, imagination, and courage.

CONTENTS

ACKNOWLEDGMENTS

I am deeply indebted to my husband, Rick McMahan, my son, Michael McMahan, and my mother, Margaret Wickes, who have supported my writing and me throughout my life.

Jerry Jenkins gave me the tools and motivation to keep writing. He is a master at writing books and teaching others how to keep readers turning the page.

Determine the thing can and shall be done and then find the way.
—Abraham Lincoln

CHAPTER 1

GRANDMA'S GHOST

Montray, Virginia, July 2022

The unforeseen move left Kelly Hamilton grasping for answers. Exhausted, she flopped into the chair while her brother, Brandan Hamilton, lifted an antique trunk from the moving van and dropped it on the porch, rattling the rocker and her nerves. The doctor after Grandpa's triple bypass warned them not to let him lift over ten pounds.

Grandpa Jeremiah Stockwell excelled as an artist, chemist, museum curator, and chef. The aroma of tomato sauce wafted into the dining room and drew Kelly to the dinner table. Her stomach growled, reminding her breakfast had occurred ages ago. The spindle-back armchair creaked as Brandan pulled it closer to his plate as generous portions of spaghetti appeared.

"Change is painful," the elderly man said, patting her arm. "Ruthie spilled what happened at the National Gymnastics Championship. You fight and forgive, Kelly. My daughter won't stay angry."

Kelly tried not to think about her mother slamming the hatchback, crushing everything she took for granted, and leaving her suspended in midair with only faith to guide her to safety. The fights, running away, getting attention had become a way of life. So why did this hurt so much?

"Eat! The pandemic drove large numbers to starvation. Don't waste a morsel. Tomorrow we'll go to the museum. Wait until you see the Civil

War artifacts I discovered," said her grandfather, the one person she trusted to be there for her no matter what.

Kelly nodded, handed Brandan the garlic bread, and enjoyed the enticing flavors. Grandpa scooped ice cream into bowls. His shaky hands sent a spoonful sailing, which landed in her lap.

"When you're done with dessert, unpack and organize your rooms. Your grandma likes the place neat." He refused to acknowledge the ice cream mishap despite repressed giggles, so Kelly hid the frozen boulder in her napkin. He held a distant expression consumed inside him. Something important pressed on his mind, but his secretive nature assured her it'd be a long time before she found out what it was.

"Can't we get the evening off to relax? Grandma's not here," said Brandan.

"That's what you think," said Grandpa, excusing himself and disappearing into his study, shaking his head.

"Ow!" Brandan scowled. "Why did you kick me? Aren't I injured enough from unloading the truck and carrying luggage up those narrow steps to our godforsaken rooms?"

"Idiot! My foot only brushed you. Grandpa misses her, and so do I," replied Kelly.

"Four years later, and he thinks his wife's in the kitchen. How can he believe that? I sat forever on those hard wooden benches at her Quaker funeral in Leesville, and I saw her laid to rest in the cemetery. We put flowers on her grave countless times, and our mom still grieves her mother's loss," said Brandan.

"What if Grandma's spirit is watching over us?"

"My sister, the seer," said her older sibling as he rolled his eyes, collected the dishes, and retired to his room. She found dishtowels stuffed under a plastic container full of paints and brushes in the kitchen.

Talk of Grandma's soul brought memories of a warm and wonderful woman. Bare, yellowed light bulbs cast strange patterns on the linoleum. A musty odor contributed to the unsettling atmosphere. Pipes rattled and spit as Kelly twisted the porcelain faucet. She shoved the screen door over the warped plank into the mudroom and let out a deep sigh. A lamp hung off a pole to light her path through the garden. The pump in the courtyard sprayed into the bucket, soaking her apron as she pushed honey-blonde bangs off her forehead.

The screen door stuck, causing her to trip, plopping a puddle near the sink. Her arms ached as she scraped dried food and dipped the plates to rinse them, often peering behind her. A night owl screeched in the nearby woods, making her drop a glass. She sensed a presence and turned as an eerie shadow bent and expanded across the cupboard with the rising moon.

"Grandma? Gram?"

Hours later, exhausted from straightening her room, Kelly collapsed into the freezing sheets, shivering. The pendulum of the grandfather's clock in the library echoed a count toward midnight, lulling her into an uneasy sleep.

The following day, a carton tumbled onto the museum driveway, spilling cans of soup and vegetables. Her arms throbbed between the moving van yesterday and unpacking the gallery truck. A restless sleep with dreams of Grandma attempting to contact her left her woozy. She bent to chase a can of corn that rolled into a small shack that served as a community food shelf. Grandpa rarely sheltered in place during COVID-19; while Kelly's personal ambitions and problems consumed her. She realized how self-absorbed her life had been during the worst of the outbreak. The National Gymnastics Competition 2022 for fourteen-year-olds became her beacon to fight against the isolation. She practiced tumbling and sent videos until the invitation arrived, announcing she made the finals in Washington, DC. The gold medal was within her reach—until her mom ruined everything.

"Run the groceries to the food shelf and set the boxes in my workroom. I'll sort things afterward. Wait until you see my latest acquisitions." Grandpa slid the heavy gates of the round barn until they thudded against the weathered siding.

Kelly continued to stack crates of food on the empty shelves while her cranky sibling piled the antiques near the entry. Relieved to hear the tailgate clang shut behind her, she lugged the last shipment into the office and collapsed in a cushioned rocker. Her brother tripped and knocked three boxes on her foot, startling her.

"Where did he go?" asked Brandan, piling the spilled artifacts on the desk. "He's been acting funny and on edge."

"I noticed it too. This is something bigger than the two of us. Let's try the basement." Kelly, curious what he wanted to show them, circled past the artwork and found her way to the staircase. Weaving looms and fabrics overflowed the space beneath the top floor. Her brother nudged her to walk faster as she descended, holding on to the winding wrought iron railing. She stopped on the step before the ground floor, horrified at the sight. Brandan pushed her aside, causing her to stumble on hard cement littered with Civil War banners, rifles, and garments. Historical novels and papers crunched under her feet and forced her to catch herself on a rack once filled with uniforms.

The armchair in the corner creaked and swiveled. Her grandfather's watery eyes conveyed his anguish and dismay. She reached for his trembling hand and offered to help him stand.

"This place is a disaster. I know I locked both doors. What have I landed myself into this time?" said Grandpa. His sigh drew short, shallow breaths. Kelly worried he was hyperventilating.

"Burglars? What's so valuable?" Brandan said as he righted a lamp and replaced a pile of volumes on the shelf before he disappeared into the back room. He returned moments later with a broken padlock and crowbar, as splinters of wood cascaded to the floor.

"Why did they tear this place apart? What did they hope to find?" Grandpa closed his eyes as if to think better. "The mirrored cabinet!" he said, attempting to walk without his cane.

Kelly took his arm and helped him across the room to a counter crammed with belts, buckles, pins, and cufflinks. He stretched his arm through the debris to clean away the glass shards.

"Lincoln's pocket watch, and coins … gone," said Grandpa.

"The watch belonged to Abraham Lincoln?" Kelly asked. Diamond and ruby rings gleamed at Kelly from the jewelry display.

"I had it authenticated along with solid gold dollars stamped with, 'Confederate States of America, 1863.' I planned on locking them in my safe, but I kept them there to show you."

"Grandpa, your wrist. It's bleeding!" Kelly grabbed a faded maroon sash with tassels and wrapped it around his fingers as a red stain emerged through the fabric.

Pale as a ghost, he clutched his chest. Kelly caught him before he could fall. She strained to understand what he tried to whisper. Her pulse quickened when she repeated his words out loud. "'My meds, jacket … Get me to the recliner!'"

His body slumped into the chair. She slipped the bottle out of the hidden inside pocket of his jacket and placed the medication under his tongue. Her fingers held pressure on his wound, but it wasn't enough to stop the bleeding. "Call for an ambulance!" she shouted to her brother in the back room.

Her brother came running and pulled out his cell phone. "No bars! I can't believe this!"

"Use the landline upstairs! Hurry!"

CHAPTER 2

THE WARNING

Two Weeks Later

Kelly, unable to sleep, wrapped the quilt snug against the cold. The nightmare of her grandfather's close call played over again in her head. His heart medication saved him from another devastating heart attack. She couldn't imagine her life without him.

Sleepiness finally took hold despite her tossing and turning. The scent of lilacs choked the air and forced her eyes open. A ghostly image of a woman inches from her face stared at Kelly. She leaped from the bed, dragging her comforter with her. Her fingers fumbled for the metal string, and light jiggled the shadows until the flowered lamp settled on.

"Grandma? It can't be you!" said Kelly.

Black silk skirts rustled toward her. As the figure got closer, a pillow skidded past her and slammed against an ornate trunk. Kelly bolted out of her room and down the hallway. She lifted the latch on her brother's door, but it was locked tight. She rattled and banged on the door. "Brandan, open your door! Help me, please! I'm scared!"

"Do you realize what time it is? Leave me alone!" he shouted.

She peered through the keyhole to see him pretending to be asleep and sighed. He had no intention of opening his door.

She hoped Grandpa was still working at his desk. Kelly hurriedly descended the narrow steps. The bedroom door flung open to an empty room. Grandpa's blazer hung on the desk chair. Ash and dead embers in the fireplace left the room cold. Before long, she slumped into a Victorian rocker, closed her eyes, and wiped a tear off her cheek.

"Where are you?" Kelly asked the empty room. A charred log rolled from the firebox, followed by a shushing sound moving in her direction. She shrieked and leaped onto a circular tabletop.

"Why are you screaming?" Her brother appeared in the doorway, squinting and rubbing his eyes.

"Stay still." Brandan moved his is finger to his lips to shush her and pointed at the table's pedestal wobbling beneath her.

The snake curled around the base as Kelly fought to maintain her balance. Jealous of his calm manner, she held her ground as Brandan grabbed a pronged stick and umbrella near Grandpa's desk. He hooked its body and pinned the brown head, pulling it free from the base of the table. She jumped down to open the patio doors and stepped aside to let her brother fling the writhing copperhead into the backyard. The glass doors slid closed with a bang.

"We moved to snake country. What happens if I'm not here?" he asked.

Kelly blocked out her brother's voice, locked the gateway to the garden, and drew the curtains tight. She hated the slimy creatures because a jealous Brandan used to tease her by tossing garter snakes at her. He informed her they were harmless, but a copperhead's venom could be deadly. She'd never forget the time she had to kill one in Stone Creek Mansion and the bloody mess it created.

"Why did you ignore me?" asked Kelly. She brushed against cobwebs and dust bunnies as she checked under the bed and dark places for lurking snakes.

"A lunatic pounded on my door. What is the matter with you?"

Grateful for Brandan's company—and the fact he had gotten rid of the snake—his insults bounced off. "I saw a ghost," Kelly said, slightly out of breath because of the adrenaline rush. A lady appeared to me dressed like she came from another century."

"Sure, and now she's in the kitchen making a cup of tea. You ought to be a fiction writer with your imagination." Her brother smirked, mocking her.

"You think because you're eighteen and two years older than me that you know everything." But in fact, she probably knew more, at least when it came to the future. Kelly shuddered, remembering the time she picked up the phone before it rang and knew her grandma had passed before anyone spoke.

"Doesn't this wretched house understand it's summer?" asked Brandan. "This chimney's unblocked because Grandpa only cared about heating his room and didn't need to bother cleaning the others."

Kelly helped her brother replace the fallen wood and added more wood to the fire. Sparks crackled and licked the logs as smoke drifted upward. Kelly felt safer, knowing snakes hated fire.

"Where *is* Grandpa?" asked Brandan.

"He hasn't been here tonight by the looks of his covers. The last time I saw him was at breakfast, when he made his famous pancakes. He mentioned he had to meet the insurance man at the museum. I sensed he was up to something," said Kelly.

"I saw him at lunchtime. He rushed past me, changed into a sweatshirt, snatched his cane, and told me not to worry because he'd be back soon."

"Did he tell you where he was going?"

"Does he ever? You know him and his secrets."

Grandpa's mysterious behavior worried Kelly. Glow lit the hearth and warmed her. Comfortable in the mohair throw, she eased into the armchair, hands still shaking. She found it hard to understand how people who lived in Virginia could accept the fact a copperhead might hide under a rock or crawl down their chimney. That thought horrified her.

"I'm staying here," said Kelly.

"Good idea. At least this way we'll stay warm, and we'll know when he gets home." Her brother stretched out, ducking under the coverlet.

Flames danced among reds and yellows, hypnotizing her. Grandpa had displayed her mounted silver medal for tumbling on the mantelpiece. She remembered standing on the podium with the reward ribbon pressed to her neck. She touched the etched surface and realized nothing could be the same. Tears streamed at the sight of her parents' empty seats. Her mother chose moments before her performance to inform her she'd left Kelly's father.

Her brother's snoring startled her. She rose, sensing a strange aura. A sorrowful weeping wrenched at her nerves. What did this spirit want? Grandpa's coat shot across the room and landed at her feet.

"Brandan, she's here! Can't you hear her?" Kelly picked up the tweed jacket and replaced it on the swivel chair.

"What?" He dragged himself from the mattress, glanced around the room, and shrugged.

"Explain how his jacket flew off the chair," ordered Kelly.

Her brother threw a log on the fire and disappeared under the blanket, leaving her on her own.

She stood still, listening for signs of the ghost hiding in the shadows. The rustle of silk and the scent of lavender stunned her senses as an icy fog passed through her, leaving her gasping for air.

CHAPTER 3

WP

The Following Day

Footsteps tramped on the porch. The screen door rattled until Kelly responded. A raven-haired boy juggled groceries that threatened to spill.

"I'm Thomas Williams from Ed's General Store. I've brought your grandfather's weekly order. Do you mind? These sacks are heavy."

Thomas rushed past her to the dining room table and set down his packages. A shiver crossed her shoulders. Kelly stared at him with a premonition about the future, but no understanding of what the impression meant. He faced her with his palm out. His blue eyes stared straight at her until her cheeks flushed when she realized what he expected. She scurried into her grandfather's bedroom to search his suit coat for loose change. A linty lozenge stuck to the fabric of his front jacket pocket and made her hand sticky. She felt a bulge in the inside pouch and found a folded sheet of paper, a gold coin, and his heart medication. Stunned by the memory of what happened to Grandpa at the museum, she dropped the bottle.

"I'm not waiting another minute," a voice came from the kitchen. "Ed will put it on your tab, and thanks for nothing!" The screen door slammed shut, followed by angry footsteps and a car revving in the driveway.

"Food," Brandan said as he picked up a pack of cookies, ripped open the package, and crammed some into his mouth.

Kelly placed the prescription bottle on the table, her hand shaking.

"Grandpa forgot his heart medication, and the doctor said he needs to carry it with him," said Kelly.

"You're joking," Brandan said, examining the bottle brimming with pills.

A coin pinged off the spindle-backed chair as she unfolded the paper and hit the Oriental rug. Brandan stopped the coin when it reeled in his direction. "Confederate States of America. This looks like a gold piece taken from the glass cabinet," said Brandan.

She smoothed the wrinkles of the paper to better see the photo of Abraham Lincoln's mirror with his double image portraying his scraggly face next to his human skull.

"Grandpa sells posters of that picture at the museum. Abe claimed his double reflection predicted his death," said Brandan as he grabbed hold of the paper and flipped it over. "It's a drawing of a covered bridge leading to an old plantation house and a porch with four columns. WP is written on the far pillar, and there's a cottage off to the side. This must be where he went."

Kelly walked past the Frank Lloyd Wright table and into the kitchen, driving memories of the hospital aside. The plastic container she'd seen her first night in Virginia no longer sat on the shelf above the sink. A chill raced down her spine. She'd been able to foresee future events since she was a little girl and was seldom wrong whenever the feeling hit her. She rushed back to find her brother.

"Remember years ago when he used his makeup kit to disguise himself as the gardener to detect who threatened him? The container of wigs, face paint, and brushes are gone. He's into something dangerous. You said he ate lunch at the diner yesterday. We have to find him," said Kelly.

"I put our bikes on the porch yesterday. It's only a mile or two to Ed's General Store. Ed may know where Grandpa went. He is Grandpa's best friend," said Brandan.

"Let's hurry. I'll follow you," said Kelly. She climbed on her ten-speed bike and pedaled close behind her brother on the well-worn path to the supermarket, shielding herself from low branches threatening to smack her in the face. The dirt transformed into mud, spraying her purple T-shirt.

Cars crowded the parking lot as she parked her bike in slats framed by carved wooden bears. A guy with black hair and tattoos covering both arms leaned against his motorcycle. She hurried, grateful to spot Thomas at the checkout counter, bagging a customer's groceries. She followed her brother past a display of oranges and grapefruits, spotting Ed at the rear of the store.

The elderly gentleman sat on a stool and organized papers on his clipboard. "Grandpa didn't come home last night, and we are worried. Have you seen him?" asked Brandan.

"Your Grandpa Jeremiah ordered lunch yesterday with a fellow I've never met." The owner stroked his salt-and-pepper beard. "I spoke to him briefly and saw him leave with the stranger."

Kelly noticed a wiry guy with chopped blonde hair and pierced earrings lurking in the adjoining aisle. He appeared to be eavesdropping on their conversation. She ignored the twitch in her shoulder and an unsettled feeling. She was more interested in what Ed had to say about her grandfather.

Brandan showed Ed the hand drawn illustration with the initials "WP" in the column. "Do you know where this is?" he asked.

Jeremiah's friend shook his head. "Sorry, kids. I'd stay far away from those places. A few years ago, a couple of nine-year-old boys explored an abandoned mansion and did not expect to fall through rotten floorboards and get killed. People claim their ghosts continue to chase each other in the third-floor hallway. Don't be foolish and try to enter one of those deathtraps."

"If you have news, you'll call?" asked Kelly.

"I'll contact you or your brother the minute I see him. I promise."

Her brother sprinted toward the exit, leaving Kelly by herself. Her stomach growled, reminding her she hadn't eaten any breakfast. The man with spiked blonde hair, which she'd noticed earlier, stood in the same spot. He spun the circular rack crammed with maps and brochures. When Kelly started walking toward him, he turned and bolted into the next aisle. Shaking off an uneasy feeling, she went to the rack and grabbed a pamphlet of noted plantations in Virginia.

Two chilled colas and two bags of chips filled her arms on her way to check out. She stood in line to pay just as the grocery clerk, Thomas Williams, the same boy who delivered Grandpa's groceries that morning, stepped outside. When he reappeared, his penetrating stare made her drop a can of soda.

"Sale on estate maps?" the dark-haired boy asked, grinning widely.

"We moved here in June and wanted to explore," said Kelly. She fumbled and spilled her purchases on the wooden checkout counter.

"I moved here a few months ago, "said Thomas. "Little did I know I traded Washington, DC for the middle of nowhere. Hope you appreciate forests, mountains, and historic ruins. Let me guess, stick it on your account?"

Her fingers touched his as he shoved the bag across the counter, sending a million butterflies flying inside her. Kelly sighed deeply, unable to figure out why she felt this way about this stranger. She tucked her grocery bag under her arm, and avoiding eye contact, raced for the exit just as the monster-sized motorcycle blasted in a thunderous cloud and vanished in the distance. Moments later, a smaller motorcycle appeared from the other side of Ed's General Store and zoomed past her.

She handed her brother the pamphlet.

"What took so long? Glad you took time to flirt with the clerk," said Brandan, grabbing the pamphlet from her hand.

"I was not flirting," answered Kelly, feeling her cheeks burn, contradicting her words.

"Then why are your cheeks red?"

Brandan spread the map on the gravel. Kelly clutched the corner against the stiff breeze and helped him search for a match to their grandpa's drawing.

"There are no covered bridges in Montray, Virginia. There's a Wildwood Plantation in the next village. WP!" He jumped to his feet and removed the ten-speed from the bike rack, leaving Kelly sitting on the gravel.

A draft hooked the edge and sent the brochure sailing. Kelly snatched the map, jumped on her bike, and pumped fast to catch up with her brother. Three miles later, legs aching, she arrived at the Leesville Quality Market.

"Google Maps show the path follows the river and leads to a footbridge," said Brandan. He cut across the street without waiting for her and disappeared past the fire station.

She made sure the items from Grandpa's jacket were still in her pocket and tried to catch Brandan. Wind brushed against her bangs, and the mist dampened her clothes. An earthy scent grew stronger the deeper she pedaled into the forest. The trail curled through wet brush, ascended steep hills, and twisted along the bank. After a while, Kelly dismounted her bike and mopped the moisture from her forehead. The dappled light darkened, making it harder to avoid the roots. She caught her breath and got back on her bike. She gripped her fingers on the handlebars and raced through the dense woods.

The path veered from a giant flat rock and forked in two distinct directions. The curved lane steered her to a dead end, proving she had no control over her predictions. If she did, she'd have known the correct route. She strained to remember landmarks until she located the leveled stone. Kelly pushed against the pedals to make up lost time. She eventually found her brother resting on a granite outcropping.

"What took so long? I thought you got eaten by a bear," Brandan said.

"Are you getting the idea no one's taken this path since the previous century?" asked Kelly between quick breaths.

"No kidding." Brandan wiped the sweat with his sleeve and gulped most of his water jug.

"Grandpa made his way through this mess?" Kelly asked, trying to imagine him struggling with his cane, tripping on fallen logs, and stepping in ruts.

"No, it would have taken him forever. He must have found a different route. The weather forecast predicts the brunt of the storm hitting us in fifteen minutes. It has taken us an hour to get this far. This paper map shows the covered bridge is close, and the mansion lies beyond it."

Kelly shook her head as he vanished through a birch grove. Drops of rain pelted her helmet and forced her to grip the handlebars so tight her knuckles turned white as she steered through the muddy path. She circled the protruding rock and found him standing under the arched ceiling of a covered bridge.

"No cell signal and my battery died. You better hurry and park your wheels under cover," said Brandan.

A flash lit up the woodland, followed by a crashing thunder. Her bicycle squeaked and moaned as she wheeled it across brittle planks. Gusts and rainfall battered the surfaces. Splashes of wetness leaked through the roof's cracks, and thunderbolts exploded too close for comfort. Brandan sat under the overhang. Her energy drained, she grabbed the snacks from her basket and sank next to him.

"Someone else knows about this path," said Brandan, pointing at a faint imprint. Kelly surveyed the muddy path surrounded by red spruce trees until she spotted fresh footprints half concealed under matted pine needles.

"These footprints go both ways," Brandan noted.

"What is on the other side of this hill?" asked Kelly.

"According to the map you picked up, Wildwood Plantation is over the rise."

Kelly finished her bag of chips and waited for the storm to pass. Downpour buffeted the roof until the sun shone patches of sunbeams through dripping leaves. She leaned her bike against the side of the covered bridge next to her brother's, planning to come back for it later. She followed Brandan, sidestepping the footprints. Musky air filled her lungs as she climbed and trudged through overgrown weeds to the crest of the hill. The road leveled and wove past a field of chickweed and wild violets. Towering oak trees bordered a regal drive, their branches intertwined into a canopy. Crows cawed in the treetops. Dampness clung to her skin, and a shiver crossed her shoulders. She tried to ignore the uncontrollable sensation foreshadowing her second sight. Powerless to control her gift, she closed her eyes and listened. A chorus of crickets couldn't hide the sound of footsteps crunching behind her, getting closer. Kelly threaded her way through the trees into the meadow.

"Brandan!" she shouted over her shoulder. "Run!"

CHAPTER 4

WILDWOOD CEMETERY

Kelly raced across the meadow, making a trail through purple wildflowers. She climbed the small hillside on the far end of the field. Holding her side, she collapsed into the crabgrass.

Brandan glowered at her as he scaled the grassy slope and brushed off his denims. "What happened?"

"I heard someone stomping through the brush and breathing hard climbing the hill from the covered bridge. Everything in me told me we're in danger."

"Did you see who?"

"No. They got too close, and I panicked."

"We crossed a snake-infested field with only my Scout knife?" Brandan asked, clearly disgusted with her.

Kelly gulped, forgetting about the snakes. She felt a greater danger and rose to make sure no one had followed. Convinced she'd lost them, Kelly discovered a well-worn path on the other side of the hill. Mud soaked her shoes as the sprawling ivory mansion sat before her in a ghostly fog, a testament to life spanning centuries. She'd give anything to know what happened to the people who lived there. Brandan skidded and clung to Kelly's shoulder, making her stumble. She grabbed his hand to keep from slipping and stood with her mouth open at the sight of an ornate eight-foot high fence, spiked arrows and pikes across the top. The overgrown path slapped her knees as she made her way to the massive gate.

Her shoulder ached pushing past the weeds that held the iron door in place. She was grateful for her brother's help. The door opened wide enough to squeeze through and into a graveyard. She wondered if their presence disturbed the souls laid to rest there. Free of premonitions and spirits, she let out an enormous sigh and stooped to read the scattered gravestones: "Louis Palmer Thompson, state leader and trusted friend of Abraham Lincoln. Died 1921; Anna Margaret, beloved wife and mother, died 1918; Alan Walters Thompson, son of Louis and Anna, died 1962."

The back fence was crowded with Queen Anne's lace and wild violets. A headstone hidden beneath a tangle of Virginia creeper caught her foot. Her nails clogged with dirt as she freed the granite headstone and read: "Josephine Virginia Thompson, beloved wife." She searched for the broken piece. The man who built Wildwood Plantation wed twice!

A crow broke the silence as a blast of air whirled and blew over the memorials. The wrought iron door clanged shut, startling her to drop the stone.

"You're kidding me! We're locked in! Someone intentionally locked the gate," Brandan said as he kicked the metal base and slumped to the ground, holding his toes. "Got any brilliant ideas? There's still no cell service. Why don't you take a running start and vault to the other side?"

Kelly rolled her eyes. "That's ridiculous! It might be possible to climb the fence. We have to try." Her feet clung on the crossbar while her fingers gripped the two-inch vertical slat. The sharp spike cut into her palm, and she dropped, falling into a thick patch of clover. Her hands trembled as she glanced upward at the high walls. She wiped the perspiration off her forehead and paced back and forth. *Who locked us in, and why?* She wondered. Kelly counted the footholds leading to the top of the gate. "I have an idea. Take off your shirt."

"What?" Brandan asked, his expression full of disgust.

"Throw it over the spikes," Kelly said. "It's our only way to escape."

Her brother stared at her for a long time. Finally, he shrugged and pulled off his shirt. Kelly spotted him from the ground. He climbed part way, tossed his shirt over the spikes, and dropped to the ground.

"Your turn," said Brandan.

Kelly left her brother standing near a gravestone, climbed skyward, and dismounted on the other side with a stuck landing. But the padlock held tight, and her idea of unlocking the gate for her brother faded. Brandan's complaints grew louder as he climbed over the sharp pikes, grabbed his shirt, and tumbled after her, falling on his backside. She helped him to his feet and wove her way through the wet grass to the path. Her brother huffed at her heels, sputtering.

Kelly sprinted down the hill, staying on the drier parts. Curls of white clouds encompassed the peaks of the Blue Ridge Mountains and touched the pine trees surrounding the plantation. The damaged shutters and peeling paint dared her to walk closer and filled her with foreboding. A faint light flickered in an upstairs bay window. Kelly swore she saw someone staring through the glass.

Warnings blended into the whistling wind as she moved toward the sagging veranda. Four columns stretched upwards twenty-five feet. Clapboards no longer exhibited their color, faded along with the memories of those who once lived there.

"Someone is tracking us. They locked us in the cemetery, and now we are entering this creepy place?" Brandan asked, holding his chest, panting.

Kelly's belly tightened and a shiver crossed her shoulders. But she had no time for her premonitions. The weathered doors groaned and creaked as she, with Brandan's help, pulled hard to open them. Her footsteps echoed across the marble floor. Dust and mold forced a cough. Dim rays of light peeked through the boarded windows, while shadows blanketed the murky corners, making her uneasy. Kelly found matches tucked into the base of a candelabrum on the fireplace mantle and lit the candles, illuminating the portrait of a forgotten Union soldier from the Civil War.

"Why would a portrait of a Union soldier be hanging in a southern plantation?" Kelly asked.

"Because both Confederate and Union sympathizers lived in northern Virginia during the Civil War," Brandan explained, climbing the grand staircase to the first balcony. Seconds later, Kelly heard the banister wobble as he slid and sent squeaks from his sneakers. "Too dark!"

"Admit it. You saw a ghost!" Kelly said, laughing at the sight of her brother getting spooked, especially after all his teasing and disbelief in her second sight.

"Shush! Do you hear that?" he asked, gripping the banister's ornate knob at the bottom of the stairs.

A silvery mist cast light on her brother. A translucent woman in black materialized on the staircase, the same apparition who appeared in her grandfather's house. Kelly's smile evaporated. *How do I tell him there is a spirit hovering right behind him,* she wondered. Icy fingers stroked her bare arm, sending an electric current pulsing through her entire body. Kelly jumped from the piano bench and ran. An agonizing moan faded behind her. The floorboards squeaked as Brandan followed her. She slammed the heavy doors and inhaled the fresh air.

"You scared me to death. What happened?" asked Brandan, pacing across the length of the porch.

"There are two lost souls haunting this place. I felt a strong connection between them. The lady in black from Grandpa's house stood behind you on the staircase, while a vile and evil spirit stroked my arm! I sensed rage, a horror so terrible I couldn't breathe!" Kelly shuddered and covered her face, trying to forget.

"This is unbelievable! You're telling me I stood inches away from one of your spooks?"

"Be glad you didn't meet the other spirit. We've got to find Grandpa before it is too late!"

"What if we are already too late?" Brandan asked.

"Don't say that! Everything in me says you're wrong."

"Kelly, behind you!" shouted Brandan.

She turned to find a tall man in overalls walking up the steps to the mansion.

"You're trespassing on private property," the gray-haired old man told them.

"Who are you?" Kelly asked, recognizing something familiar about him.

"Henry Barnett. I'm hired to guard Wildwood Plantation until the real estate office sells it. They had a buyer, but he realized the cost of making repairs and reconsidered. I have to ask you to come with me to the cottage. I'm calling my friend, Sheriff Martin, to take you home. It's for your own safety."

"We're trying to find our grandfather, who didn't return home last night," Kelly explained. "We think he came here. He has a heart condition and forgot his medication."

"Sorry, but my orders are to keep people away from here. I will let the sheriff know your situation, and he can investigate further. Please follow me," said Henry.

"Why should we follow you? You're a complete stranger," Brandan said, a scowl on his face.

"How do we know you are telling us the truth?" Kelly asked. She stood defiantly with her hands on her hips.

"Your parents taught you well," said Henry.

Kelly stepped back as the caretaker reached into his pocket and pulledout his ID and a letter of instructions from the real estate office. Convinced the stranger told the truth, she followed him off the porch. Still shaky from being touched by evil, Kelly welcomed the chance to catch her breath. But she had no intention of going home.

The gravel drive curled toward a cottage. Kelly smacked her knee on a massive bumper protruding from the caretaker's oversized Silverado truck. He led them further down the road and into the cabin. She let her body sink deep into the sagging brown leather couch.

"You two have no business here. This relic threatens to fall in on itself," said the old man, disappearing into the kitchen.

"Kelly, we're in trouble," said Brandan flinging his arms upward and knocking over a pile of Civil War books on the coffee table.

Henry reappeared in the doorway with a beige receiver tucked against his ear. "I need to speak with Sheriff Martin Lane." He motioned for Brandan to pick up the Civil War books and replace them on the coffee table and returned to the kitchen.

Kelly scanned the room for any means of escape. "Brandan, Grandpa's cane is in the umbrella stand! Proof he came to Wildwood Plantation. We have to go back into the mansion and find him."

A blast of air poured through an open window, forcing her to push her hair from her eyes. The caretaker's conversation with the sheriff drifted into the room, leaving them unguarded. Kelly motioned toward the open window and waited for Brandan to crawl through first. She crouched low and swung her leg over the windowsill. A nail caught her sleeve as she squeezed through the opening and dropped next to her brother. The wet grass penetrated the fabric on her knees. They hadn't gotten far when she overheard a voice and paused under a dogwood tree.

"Never mind, Martin, they've gone," said the caretaker in an angry tone. "I'll let you know when I find them."

CHAPTER 5

THE HAUNTING

Kelly crawled around hedges and trees without drawing attention. A blue jay chimed in branches, and a breeze buffeted their leaves, but there was no sign of the caretaker. She didn't trust the police to find Grandpa. What could have happened to him?

She passed by a metal door covered in tangled green vines. "You think that's a way into the mansion?" asked Kelly.

"The overgrown ivy shows no one's opened it in years. I found a better way," answered Brandan. Kelly stepped back as he tugged on the handle, releasing the bulkhead doors.

She threw off a chill, damp from the rain and mud, and followed her brother into the mansion, avoiding stepping on twisted metal and rotting wood. The cement staircase crumbled, sending bits of stone cascading downward and bouncing off the bottom step. Sunlight diminished, but not before she noted steps leading to the first floor. She felt her way, touching the cool surface. Her brother threw himself against the wooden door, with Kelly close behind, breaking the lock. She dodged the broken tiles as they entered the kitchen.

Searching the rooms on the first floor revealed abandoned fireplaces, fallen plaster, and stained, peeling wallpaper, but no sign of Grandpa.

"This manor gives me the creeps," said Brandan.

"Why did Grandpa leave his cane in the caretaker's cottage? He drew the map for us to find; I'm sure of it. Where did he go?" asked Kelly.

"He has to be here," answered her brother. "We need more light. I'm going to open the shutters upstairs."

The candelabrum illuminated the portrait of Union officer Louis Palmer Thompson, proud and entitled, but not evil. The wick floated on the wax and threatened to extinguish itself. Dancing shadows warned her to move, remembering the evil spirit's touch. Stairs creaked, increasing panic with each step. She sensed someone staring at her from below. The hairs on the back of her neck tingled as she whirled to witness a silvery sphere lingering at the bottom of the stairwell. The white orb transformed into the same spirit who visited her in Grandpa's room. Anna, or perhaps Josephine Thompson, now buried in the cemetery, wanted her attention and followed her like she expected her to do something. When the woman's gentle whine shifted to sobs, Kelly jumped two steps at a time to the second-floor balcony.

"Did you hear her?" asked Kelly.

"Who?" Her brother's eyes narrowed, mocking her.

"You know who!"

"I'm listening to my ear buds to cancel sounds," said Brandan.

"Scarier to not know who's coming," said Kelly.

He pulled the flimsy wire from his ears. "Thanks a lot." He yanked open the shutters, pouring light onto the second-floor landing.

Kelly dodged the rotting steps and trailed behind her brother to the third floor. She helped pound the latch loose and pulled until the shutters sprang open, slamming into the wall. Light flooded the platform, revealing floating particles that forced her to cover her face.

She retraced her steps to the second floor, sidestepped the splintered wood, and glanced over her shoulder. But the diffused daylight made it difficult to tell if a spirit had followed her. The second-floor master bedroom, covered in mold and dust, signaling it had been emptied of furniture long ago, offered no clues. Moldy splotches seeped out of the decaying flowered wallpaper, prompting her to gag. Hangers rattled in the walk-in closet, and an angled door led to an oval bathroom with a claw-foot tub. A premonition threatened to unnerve her when she touched the rusty shower curtain rings and saw two beetles crawling through rancid-smelling debris. She spun toward the sound of dripping water and turned the faucet handle until water soaked her hands.

"Brandan, this place has running water! Someone didn't bother to shut off the faucet."

"The water flows from a well. I don't like this. More tricks from the creep who locked the cemetery gate. I'll wait for you in the next room," said her brother and disappeared through the bedroom door into the hallway.

Kelly slammed the bathroom door behind her, holding on to the reason she came to Wildwood Plantation. She felt someone watching her. The hallway floor squeaked with each step, rattling her nerves. She passed a row of empty rooms until she heard sounds drifting from an open door. There she found her brother sitting in a captain's chair amid the dark-paneled walls of the study. The roll top desk with bookshelves attached on either side offered no clues. Her brother stood to examine the small drawers and hidden panels, while Kelly plunked into the chair and attempted to open the larger drawer under the desktop. It stuck halfway. Fresh fingerprints pressed into the thick dust showed someone had opened the drawer recently. She found a rectangular metal piece wedged in the crack and freed it with her fingernails.

Her brother grabbed the tag from her hand and carried it to the window.

"You found a daguerreotype," said Brandan.

"A what?"

"An old-fashioned photograph," Brandan said as he handed her the picture.

She recognized Louis Thompson in a blue uniform with his first wife. "Josephine's the lady in black!" She stuffed the daguerreotype into her pocket, resolved to find out more.

"Why is she sobbing?" asked Brandan.

"You heard her! Admit it."

His smirk continued to deny the spirit world and his sister's sensitivity. Kelly knew whether or not he denied believing in premonitions, a part of him questioned it.

She followed her brother to the nursery. Her foot caught on the fallen plaster in the door frame. "Kelly, be careful!" Brandan shouted, inching his way against the wall to the exit. She reached for his hand and pulled him to safety.

"That was close," said Kelly, feeling her heart pounding in her chest.

She kept close to her brother as they explored the last three rooms on the second floor, keeping aware of the danger. Bay windows flooded the bedroom at the end of the hall with light. Kelly rushed toward the telescope, which was mounted on a tripod. She peered through the lens and positioned the spyglass to find a full view of the drive, meadow, and cemetery hill.

"What's going on here?" asked Brandan.

"Two motorcycles are leaning against an oak tree. I recognize the Harley from Ed's parking lot. Those are the same flame decals that thundered from the parking lot, spraying gravel everywhere," said Kelly.

Her brother nudged her aside and accidentally hit her arm as he swiveled the telescope across three glass panes. She stood beside him and stared through the window at the lengthy drive and cemetery hill.

"They watched us cross the meadow from this window and waited, knowing the right moment to lock us in the graveyard. The man on the Harley has tattoos covering both arms. I bet the smaller motorcycle belongs to the wiry boy with a spiked blond hair. He eavesdropped on our conversation with Ed. I sensed a dark aura when I got near him. He made the hair on my neck stand on end," said Kelly.

"What do they want?" Her brother grimaced, stomping hard as he hit the wall with his fist.

"Careful of the rotten …" Kelly warned, but not in time. Boards shattered beneath Brandan. Kelly grabbed his hand as he careened to the floor. She pressed her leg against the distant surface, straining to hold on as her foot jammed into a splintered board. Brandan's grasp slipped through her fingers. His scream made Kelly's heart sink as he crashed below. The commotion stirred the dust and settled into pitch-blackness.

"Brandan?"

A frightening silence drifted through the gloom, disturbed by a harsh moaning rising from the corridor. Trembling, Kelly struggled in vain to free herself. The mournful cries grew louder and closer.

"Help!" Kelly screamed until a shiver crossed her shoulders and she turned. A man in a Confederate uniform materialized in front of her. Seconds later, the ghostly vision howled in pain as blood oozed out of his chest.

Kelly shrieked as the blood vanished from his uniform, exposing a hole in his chest. The spirit's body floated within inches of her before it blended into a dark corner. Her foot wedged tight, and a sharp splinter threatened to slice into her bone. The silence was disturbed by the sound of footsteps approaching from the hallway.

"Brandan?"

Powerful fists caught her, yanking her to safety, and sending her shoe tumbling below, landing with a thud. Trembling, she turned to face the caretaker and rubbed her sore ankle.

"I told you not to poke around this place. Where's the other kid?" he asked, stroking his gray beard and shaking his head.

"He slipped through the floorboards and doesn't answer!" Kelly said, grateful to hear the custodian's gravelly voice. "How did you find me?"

"Blood-curdling screams pinpointed your exact location and made me think somebody tried to hurt you. Call me Henry."

"The rotten boards threatened to crumble, and I panicked," said Kelly. She kept the appearance of the bloody ghost to herself, not wanting it to be real. She accompanied her rescuer past several empty rooms to the ballroom. Eerie mist shrouded the cloakroom. Henry lifted a stool to smash the boarded window. Rays streamed into the room, revealing broken ceiling tiles scattered below the second-floor alcove where her brother fell.

Henry sorted through fragments, lifted the layers, and walked to the exit. "No traces except these drag marks. It's possible he didn't walk out on his own."

"Where is he?" Kelly shook the debris off her sneaker, slipped her foot inside, and tied the laces tight.

"He wandered dazed, or somebody captured him," answered Henry, pushing the fallen support beams aside.

His words circled in her mind. She did not want to believe any of the events of the past few hours happened. "You think my brother dragged himself to the door because he hurt himself?"

"Hard to know," answered Henry.

"How do we find him? Why doesn't he answer?" Kelly wiped a tear from her cheek.

"My friend will help. Last I checked, Martin's delayed with an emergency. I'll be back after I try the sheriff's office again. Try not to panic. You'll wake up the dead."

Kelly wondered if he knew of her psychic abilities but dismissed the idea.

"Ow! Stupid slab," she said, kicking a support beam. Her premonitions occurred when she least expected them. Something glinted beneath layers, giving her hope of a clue. She dug, tearing with her nails while pieces of white plaster hit the side wall, until she held Brandan's Scout knife in her hands. Splinters and broken bits evidenced a struggle as she slid her brother's knife into her sock and feared the worst. Her sigh filled with dread as she left the room where Brandan fell and entered the ballroom. Shadows pierced the cracks, painting uneven streaks on the hardwood floor with no sign of anyone.

"He promised to return, and I refuse to wait another minute," she said to the portrait of Officer Thompson.

The massive entryway creaked under her feet as she fled the mansion steps and raced past the caretaker's monster truck to his cabin. A squeaky screen door announced her presence in the living room. She stepped over strewn papers and righted a lamp. The kitchen door swung open part way, forcing her to stumble over the caretaker, who was tied to a padded chrome chair.

"What happened?" she asked, ripping off the duct tape that covered his mouth and cutting the ropes with a sharp kitchen knife.

"Two hooded men jumped me, hit me with a cane, and knocked me unconscious. I awoke and found myself bound to this chair. I waited an eternity for you to realize I wasn't coming back, but when you didn't show, I thought they nabbed you too!"

A cut wire dangled from the dead wall phone. The caretaker checked the bars on the cell phone in his shirt pocket. She replaced the receiver and tried her cell.

"Don't Bother. No service." He rubbed his wrists, glugged a bottle of water, and paced as he told her what happened.

"The older guy with tattoos on both arms threatened me. The younger kid called him Eric and pleaded with him not to hurt me. When the boy complained, Eric slapped him hard."

"They left Ed's General Store minutes ahead of Brandan and me, and we found their motorcycles near the drive," said Kelly. "Do you think they kidnapped my brother? What about Grandpa? What do they want?"

"You have reason to worry. I surprised the two of them in my cottage stuffing journals, books, and maps into a canvas bag while they grilled me about the information I gathered. They'll hurt anyone who prevents them from accomplishing their mission."

"What mission?"

"To uncover secrets and riches of the past," Henry said, his voice trailing off as he winced and grabbed his forehead with both hands.

She picked up Grandpa's cane on the linoleum floor and noticed blood on the handle.

"You're bleeding," Kelly said.

"Hand me the first aid kit in the drawer next to the refrigerator."

Kelly waited while he disinfected and bandaged his head before she dared to ask him more questions. "We can't wait for the sheriff. What if Brendan is seriously hurt? Help me search. You know this place better than I do."

Henry nodded and used the back of his chair to help him stand. She sensed his anxiety. But something familiar about his caring eyes made her trust him.

She followed Henry to the mansion and through the heavy doors into the main room. Kelly sighed deeply as she realized the rooms on the first floor offered no clues to the whereabouts of her grandfather or brother.

Henry stood beside her in the kitchen and shook his head. "We're not giving up. I promise. But I need you to answer a question. Why did you go back into the mansion when I told you of the danger?"

Kelly hooked the cane on the chair back, sighed, and wrung her hands. She leaned against the dusty counter. "When Grandpa didn't return home, I found his prescription bottle, a Confederate coin, and this poster of the Abraham Lincoln with a map on the other side leading to this mansion. He needs his medication to prevent another heart attack, and I need to find my injured brother."

"Since we haven't anything to go on so far, let's review what I know," said Henry, stroking his beard. "The book the culprits stole from my cottage was Louis Thomas's journal. Lincoln worked with a detective, Allan Pinkerton, and Major Thompson to build a secret shelter in an old copper mine that runs underneath the mansion. Lincoln received constant death threats during the Civil War and needed somewhere to hide with his wife, Mary Todd Lincoln, if things became too dangerous."

Kelly remembered the daguerreotype and drew it from her pocket. "Louis's first wife?"

The caretaker studied the photo and nodded. "A brave woman."

"I hear her crying. What happened to her?"

"Louis and Josephine married in 1860. A few years later, a starving prisoner of war named Ambrose escaped. The couple was enjoying a summer's day on the portico when the Confederate soldier surprised them. Josephine leaped from the porch swing in front of the bullet meant for her husband and died. Louis blew a hole through the officer's chest before he reloaded."

Henry's story gave her goose bumps. She closed her eyes, hoping to forget the sight of blood pouring from Ambrose's chest. "Josephine materializes to me, but I'm at a loss to know what she wants," said Kelly.

A loud creak and shuffling noises made her whip around toward the pantry. She handed Henry a broken table leg to knock the corroded latch free. He hauled a young man from his hiding spot.

"Thomas?" Kelly dropped her jaw in disbelief. "What are you doing here?" She stepped aside as Henry seized one of Thomas's hands and twisted it behind him.

"Take it easy. I grew restless in an empty store. Ed let me go. I overheard your plans in the parking lot," said Thomas.

"Empty your pockets," Henry ordered, releasing the boy's wrist.

Thomas dumped loose change, a packet of gum, and a thick folded paper on to the counter.

"What are you doing, hiding in the pantry?" asked Henry. "Answer me!"

"I followed Kelly and her brother. I had nothing better to do."

Kelly unfolded the thick linen paper. It was a blueprint of Wildwood Plantation. "This diagram shows three floors and the location of every room in the mansion. You relied on this map to follow and taunt us?" asked Kelly. "You're the one who locked us in the graveyard!" Her eyes narrowed as her fingers clenched. She slammed her fist against the cabinet.

"Moaning from underneath the staircase added to the effect, and I especially liked it when you vaulted over the eight-foot gate."

"My brother fell through rotten boards and disappeared. Did that thrill you too?" Kelly bristled at his smirk.

Henry signaled her to calm herself. It was a motion that looked familiar.

Thomas turned to face her from a distance. Kelly's cheeks burned.

"I didn't hurt anyone," said Thomas.

"Do you know where my brother and grandpa are?"

"Not sure."

Kelly exchanged looks with Henry. Clenching her jaw, she motioned toward the kitchen door and followed the rat through the corridor and into the main hall.

"Whether or not you believe me, I'm sorry about your brother," Thomas said a serious expression on his face.

Kelly closed her eyes and turned away.

"Wait here. I'll check this guy's story. I don't trust him," said Henry. The caretaker and Thomas left Kelly in the main hall and disappeared into the drawing room. Moments later, the double doors slid shut.

Kelly sat at the grand piano, tapping her fingers. She remembered the blueprint of the mansion and unfolded it on the piano lid. The diagram displayed three floors and a basement. The right corner flap hid the faded initials LB, and a few rooms had funny markings. A shiver ran down her back, and she returned the map to her back pocket.

A white cloud floated on the staircase, transforming into the woman in her photograph. *What now?* Kelly wondered. The ghostly spirit drifted closer, setting her teeth on edge. Kelly sprang from the bench and slid the drawing room doors open to discover an unconscious Thomas and no sign of the caretaker.

CHAPTER 6

THE NORTH STAR

"Thomas, wake up!" Kelly shook his shoulders, but Thomas lay still on the tattered carpet. Rustling noises and muffled voices floated into the room from behind the fireplace. Her knees scraped the rough surface as she crept closer, held her breath, and leaned against the wall to hear what they were saying.

"She's persistent. How do we take care of her?" Kelly heard faintly. She cupped her hand and pressed her ear harder to the wall hoping to amplify their voices.

"I haven't decided. This is our chance to score big, and I'm not letting her, her brother, or anyone else get in our way. Find her!" ordered a man in a gruff voice.

"Eric, nothing's gone as we planned," said a younger voice.

"Willie, I've taken care of you your whole life, so shut up and hold his arm."

The mirror built above the mantle showed her face, frozen with terror. Scuffling noises quieted, but Kelly lingered a long while before turning back to Thomas. She scrambled across the drawing room floor and moved him behind a paisley loveseat. His breath felt moist in her palm as she covered his mouth, listening for any signs of the two men returning. She helped Thomas sit upright and leaned him against the upholstery.

"Ooh, what happened?" Thomas moaned, rubbing his skull.

"Two men tied the caretaker to a chair in his cottage. I released him, but he's been recaptured. And now they're searching for me. Didn't you see them?" asked Kelly.

"The old man questioned me and headed for the fireplace. I turned to join him when something struck me from behind."

Kelly clasped his hand and helped him to his feet. The warmth from his palm flowed through her, making her giddy.

"We better get out of here," said Thomas, grinning.

Kelly's heart pounded in her chest as the heavy doors creaked open. She raced toward the stone lions that guarded the mansion and crouched under the windows, staying close to Thomas. Winding through a patch of birch trees, Kelly trudged on a dirt road with fresh tire tracks.

"Kelly, check this out," Thomas said, running ahead.

Kelly found Thomas in front of an abandoned shack. The door of the deteriorating cabin swept into a veil of cobwebs and stuck to her T-shirt. Light poured through windows, exposing inches of dust on a discarded bench, which made her cough. Her sweaty hands held on to the rickety railing as she climbed the staircase after Thomas to make sure they were alone.

"Slave quarters. The walls are what's left of their bunk beds," said Thomas.

Confident no one was lurking, and uncomfortable with the ghosts of the past, Kelly made a beeline for the ground floor. She found a black wooden container on the mantle of the stone fireplace and plopped herself on a dusty pine bench to examine the box. The latch pinched her finger and refused to budge just as hands gripped her from behind.

"Ahhh!" Kelly screamed and jumped to her feet.

"Boo!" Thomas whirled around in front of her and seized the mysterious black package.

"Thanks. I'm scared out of my mind without your help," said Kelly.

"Let me," said Thomas. He yanked on the rusted clasp until it popped open. He pulled out a small, leather-bound book. "Just a stupid Bible," he said, putting the book in Kelly's hands.

The brittle pages stuck together and threatened to fall apart in her hands. The black-leather cover and damaged spine felt lumpy. "Names and dates written in tiny handwriting fill the front of this book. This is a diary of births and deaths, starting in 1820," Kelly said, unable to read a note scrawled on the last page.

Movement flashed by the front door window. "Someone's out there. They found us," Kelly said. Thomas stood near the back window and acted like he didn't hear her.

She shoved the small Bible into her pocket and dragged him outside. Wet grass soaked her shoes as she hurried to hide behind a grove of towering red oak trees mingled with pine, releasing their strong earthy scent.

Seconds later, a diesel-engine revved and smashed into the cottage, forcing the wooden cabin to lean and the chimney to snap. Loud crashing sounds hit again. The oversized pickup from the caretaker's home smashed the brittle cabin into splinters, sending a century of dirt and history into oblivion. The motor quieted, and car doors slammed as two young men investigated their devastation, pausing within yards of Kelly's hiding place.

"I noticed the caretaker hid his keys under the visor this morning when I checked out the monster truck. I never guessed we'd be using it this way. This truck plows through anything," said Willie, dripping with sweat.

"The squeaky front door and muddy footprints made it easy to find them. Willie, when you spied through the window to make sure they were inside, I figured it was a simple way to get rid of them." Kelly recognized the gruff tones of the older man from behind the fireplace.

"Eric, I don't like hurting people," said Willie.

"You might when you realize how rich we are going to be. Those two kept getting in our way and too close to figuring things out. They're dead now, and we have two fewer problems. Let's go," Eric answered, walking away.

Kelly didn't dare inhale until she heard the battered truck drive away. She stepped out to examine the ruins. Her tears spilled, wetting her face. She reached for Thomas's hand and felt outrage racing through every fiber of his being.

"They tried to kill us," said Thomas. He shook his fist at the sky and ran ahead of her.

She hurried to catch him, dodging bricks, glass, and boards filled with nails. "Take me back to the mansion," said Kelly. How close they came to being crushed to death strengthened her resolve to fight against Willie and Eric. She was determined to stop them before they harmed anyone else.

Thomas's eyes cast downward as he mumbled, "Not a good plan."

"You owe me. Please!"

He kicked a rock across the gravel drive and heaved a larger one at the debris, shattering glass shards. "We're both going to regret this," he said and motioned for her to lead.

Kelly raced toward the mansion. She paused by the stone lions to catch her breath. There had to be another way in. She crawled to the far side, ducking beneath windows, and discovered a gray door under the decking of the second-floor balcony with a sign that read, "Danger, Keep Out!"

"Don't you think the sign might be there for a reason?" asked Thomas, clasping her hands in his.

Her heart beat faster. She was drawn to him, but Eric's threats made her pull back. "This whole place threatens to fall on our heads, but it hasn't stopped us yet," Kelly answered.

"You're determined, aren't you?" Thomas let go and moved farther away from the door. Kelly held her breath as he took a running start and kicked down the brittle boards. She stepped toward the entrance, and seconds later, felt hands pull her back from a dark hole that dropped into a deep chasm.

"That was close," she said, conscious of Thomas's breath on her shoulder. Kelly turned and faced his penetrating stare, aware of his arms around her waist. He leaned in, and she felt his lips press tenderly against hers, sending a rush of excitement that filled her soul and opened her heart.

"Wow!" she said, releasing his embrace, finding it hard to breathe.

"Yea, I didn't mean for that to happen. You're safe; that's what matters," said Thomas, kicking a fallen branch off the path.

Oak trees towered next to the railing. Kelly grabbed Thomas's hand and climbed to the lower limb. Leaves and branches shook as she waited for him to reach the balcony.

"Ow!" She heard Thomas yell and scrambled to join him, making sure to place her feet on secure branches and hanging on to upper limbs. Kelly freed his shoelace, which had caught on the railing, and he landed on the deck.

She scraped her arm on a sharp branch, vaulted over the iron grill, and formed a perfect landing, smiling at Thomas's sheepish face. Their near-death experience and passionate kiss opened her heart, yet she didn't know what to do with her new feelings.

"Eight years of gymnastic tumbling. One of the few times my parents paid attention to me until the nationals, when everything fell apart," said Kelly.

"My mom is a nurse, and my old man is a middle-school history teacher. They're never home. And then without warning, they announced their great idea of buying a farmhouse in Virginia. They stole me from my life, my friends, and dumped me here," said Thomas. He pulled her close and stroked her hair. "I hated this place—until I met you."

His lips melted against hers. *How could this be happening?* Kelly wondered. She tore herself from his arms, concerned they wasted precious time.

The rusty lock on the screen door stuck fast despite her attempts. Thomas picked a loose board from the deck, pushed past her, and smashed the lock. He acted as if breaking and entering came to him naturally. A shudder crossed her shoulders as she entered the enclosed porch, dimly lit because of the overgrown ivy covering the windows.

Kelly lifted the black latch and stepped into the second-floor hallway. She held on to the white railing that curled in a circular pattern past the landing to the first floor before entering the master bedroom. She found Thomas exploring a wooden cabinet. Her lungs filled with dust and glue from the peeling flowered wallpaper. Shocked at her appearance in the mirror above the fireplace, she pulled her fingers through matted honey-blonde hair and rubbed mud off her cheeks, remembering the two men who tried to kill her.

"What are you doing?" asked Kelly.

"Searching for a secret passageway."

She spread the blueprints on the floor. He kneeled and brushed against her, causing her to lose focus.

"What are these strange tiny markings?" Kelly asked.

"The North Star with six points surrounding two longer stems marked spaces for runaway slaves to hide," he replied.

She plucked the small black book from her pocket and flipped to the back. "Here's the same symbol. But pages are missing."

"It's a slave Bible. My dad taught me the white landowners edited it to hold them in line and convince them that God condoned slavery."

"How could the owners justify treating individuals as property?"

"Slavery was once a way of life in many places."

Kelly wrung her hands. The Civil War had once been only a history lesson, but now it touched her directly. Ambrose escaped a Union prison, and she shuddered at the memory of blood pouring out of his chest. Josephine gave her life to protect her husband. Kelly hoped she'd be willing to die to save someone she loved.

"The Underground Railroad helped slaves escape to the north through Snickers' Gap, a few miles from this house. How many rooms have this symbol?" asked Thomas.

Kelly studied the diagram for another star with elongated points while Thomas paced the squeaky floorboards. She averted her eyes when he caught her staring. "There's a symbol on this floor," she said, remembering where she discovered the daguerreotype as he leaned over her shoulder.

Whispering murmurs drifted from the ash-filled grate but grew silent seconds later. "Did you hear that?" Kelly asked, clutching Thomas's sleeve.

"What?" asked Thomas.

"I thought I recognized my brother's voice."

"This was a dumb idea. If we heard them, Eric and Willie heard us," said Thomas. "I'll check to see if the coast is clear and meet you down the hall."

Eerie silence motivated her to put the blueprint in her pocket and bolt into the hallway, checking empty rooms for Thomas. A pulsing sensation passed through her hand as she touched the doorknob to the study. Bookcases still guarded either side of the desk. She sat and forced the center drawer, pushing and pulling until it slid open. A spike hung in the middle, jamming the drawer's movement and grazing the tip of her thumb. Her lips tightened with determination. She pounded the handle with her fist, but nothing happened. Closing her eyes, she reached in and pushed the toggle sideways. Kelly was startled by a grinding noise and a blast of stale air as the bookcase on the left swung open. Light illuminated a rickety staircase.

Thomas appeared, brushed by Kelly, and disappeared into the passageway, encouraging her to follow. Kelly hopped over a cracked wooden board, catching herself, and leaned on the splintered railing as an act of faith, praying that her feet would touch the next step. Eerie sensations of being watched made her shiver, but she kept moving. Thomas's voice grew louder until she found him on the first-floor landing. He clutched her hand and swung her into his arms.

"Why didn't you wait?" asked Kelly. Her eyes adjusted in the dim hallway, struggling to make peace with her misgivings. Light glowed beneath a doorway several feet to the left. She followed him into a cramped space lit by the afternoon sun. Drawn to the wardrobe in the corner by something more than curiosity, Kelly pulled the handles and discovered a secret panel opened into the kitchen. Thomas, with a sheepish grin, pushed her aside to grab a backpack wedged in the cabinet's corner.

"The caretaker yanked you from this cupboard. You hid here and lied to me this whole time. What else aren't you telling me?" Kelly asked, feeling as though her heart would explode out of her chest at his betrayal.

"Eric and Willie tried to kill you and me, remember? Shh! Listen," said Thomas, pointing to a dumbwaiter that had rotted.

Murmuring voices drifted from its shaft. She poked her head into the opening and the voices grew louder.

"You're bleeding," said a familiar voice.

"Stop fussing. I have no intention of leaving the earth in this godforsaken place."

"Brandan?" Kelly waited for the seemingly endless silence to break.

"Kelly? They locked us in a hidden room. I'm not sure where. Be careful. They hurt Grandpa, and he needs his medication. Hurry, please! I don't trust Eric. He bragged you were dead and that we're next."

CHAPTER 7

A HOUSE DIVIDED

S huffling noises and muffled voices sent her heart pounding as she waited for her brother's voice to echo through the dumbwaiter. "Those idiots checked in a minute ago. They threw the caretaker against a concrete slab, causing the guy to lose consciousness," said Brandan.

"They're dangerous. But since they think we're dead, I am safe for the moment. Here's Grandpa's heart medicine," said Kelly, dropping the prescription bottle into the abyss.

"Grandpa needs a hospital."

"I'll find you. I promise!" said Kelly.

Thomas offered her a sip of his bottled water and enveloped her in his embrace. Her heart raced until she remembered how he hid in this very room.

"We need to get out of here. All this yelling down the dumbwaiter shaft may have signaled those two idiots that we are still alive," warned Thomas as he reached into his knapsack and pulled out a flashlight.

The stilted air made it hard to breathe as she navigated the narrow passageway behind Thomas, praying she hadn't alerted Eric and Willie. The bobbing light shone on a hanging tapestry as they passed through the lengthy hallway. She stubbed her foot on a loose brick. But this time, it resulted in more than a sore foot. A secret panel scraped the floor and opened into the drawing room.

"Back where we started," said Thomas, closing the hidden panel.

"Did you witness my brother and grandpa being captured? Do you know where they are? Please, tell me the truth."

Thomas squirmed and pushed her away. "I won't apologize again. Either you trust me or you don't."

"Okay, I'm sorry." She stopped pressing the matter, remembering his passionate kiss and that Eric tried to kill him.

He stared at her a great while before he gripped her hand. "Brandan spoke underneath the dumbwaiter, so let's check the basement," said Thomas, striding to the kitchen.

Concrete crumbled with each step into the eerie gloom of the basement. Jagged boards threatened to crash from the ceiling as she leaped past piles of decaying wood. Daylight poured in from a giant hole in the landing. She inhaled the pine scent from the branches encroaching on the opening before she traversed the debris to the bottom and into pitch-dark. Thomas shone his flashlight on stone walls, rusty pipes, and a coal bin.

Kelly pressed ahead into a room of fallen bricks and cement. "This is hopeless. These rooms are plaster graveyards with no sign of Brandan and Grandpa. They aren't here."

She dusted cobwebs from her jeans and made her way back to the main hall and ballroom. Sitting on the hard bench, made her aware of the Bible sticking out of her back pocket. Tucked within its pages, Kelly found a diagram and spread it on the ballroom's piano. The North Star scrawled in the corner identified another hiding place on the third floor.

"The library connects to three floors and descends underground," said Kelly, dreading the thought of being discovered. "Why did they kidnap Grandpa and Brandan in the first place, and why did they take the caretaker?"

"One thing for sure, Eric and Willie do not care who they hurt," Thomas replied.

Kelly ascended the staircase, jumping over broken steps to the second-floor landing, where she stopped in her tracks. The sensation of being watched grew stronger. The lady in black was staring down at her from the third floor. The lady's soft crying grew louder as Thomas, oblivious to her presence, passed through her flowing skirts. Kelly helped Thomas push against the library door until it opened.

Strong rays of sunlight cascaded in the room with abundant particles of dust. She covered her nose with the collar of her T-shirt. Kelly recognized books written in the 1860s, during Lincoln's presidency as a vile arm reached through the stacks of books and touched her fingers.

"Ambrose!" she shrieked as an emaciated Confederate soldier appeared in the bookcase. A blood-curdling moan rattled the windowpanes, and a book sailed from the shelf. The door swung shut and locked, trapping her and Thomas in the library. The North Star symbol on the blueprint showed the room had a secret passageway. A book smacked her on the forehead, interrupting her search. She tossed a copy of *Jane Eyre* at the ghost, but it passed straight through him and hit the bookcase.

Kelly dodged soaring missiles and accidentally knocked against the wall lamp. A grinding sound startled her as she tripped backwards, catching herself on a dark platform. She helped Thomas through the opening and slammed the door shut just as more books banged against the wall on the other side.

"Did you have to scream?" Thomas asked.

Kelly sighed, praying no one heard, and accompanied Thomas through a sagging wooden door with rusty hinges.

Thomas handed her the flashlight and stepped into the shadows. She shined the light into the corners of the cramped, windowless space, and winced, realizing slaves hid and slept on the dark-stained mattress that lay on the floor. A drawer slammed shut, making her drop the flashlight. Kelly turned, slamming her knee against a rocking chair.

"Ow! What are you doing?" asked Kelly.

Light flooded the room. Thomas emerged from the shadows wearing a furry stove-top hat and carrying a hurricane lamp. Kelly settled into a rocking chair, shaking her head. "Where did you find the light, and what are you wearing on your head?"

"Someone left the lantern and the hat on top of the bureau. I found matches in the drawer," he replied, handing her the hat.

Kelly stroked the soft fur covering the surface. When she reached in, she found a felt rim with a silk lining on one side and a paper tucked into the brim. She unfolded the yellowed paper and leaned closer to the light. "A house divided against itself cannot stand. This government cannot endure half-slave and half-free. Did this hat belong to Abraham Lincoln?" asked Kelly.

"Lincoln's Gettysburg Address. My father told me Lincoln used to keep his notes for his speeches in the brim of his hats." Thomas grabbed the hat out of her hands.

Kelly's neck tingled with a strong premonition that led her to wrench the small leather-bound Bible from her jean's pocket. The rear cover came unglued at the top, and she retrieved two papers tucked inside.

"A blueprint for Lincoln's bunker shows four flights of stairs that descend into underground tunnels. That has to be where they are holding Grandpa, Brandan, and the caretaker!"

"What's the other note?" Thomas asked.

"A letter to Officer Thompson."

My Dear Friend Louis,

Mary and I will never forget your generosity or the times you gave me a respite from the ravages of the Civil War. My enemies have multiplied, and the shelter is a godsend when insurgents make it impossible to stay at the residence. You have my eternal gratitude.

Your friend,

Abraham Lincoln

Wooden steps creaked and moaned outside the alcove door. Thomas blew out the lantern, leaving Kelly in the dark. Kelly froze. She heard two distinct voices. Flickers of light illuminated Thomas as he slipped through the door.

How could she have been so careless, acting as if she weren't in danger? What did Thomas think he was doing? Kelly wedged between the rear of the dresser and an unfinished surface of cobwebs. She checked on the Bible, the pocket-knife hidden in her sock, and pushed her cell phone deep. Muffled voices drifted through the entryway and became clearer as the door opened a few inches.

"Hey, you have my hat. I wondered where I left it," said Willie.

"You tried to murder me. Why? I did everything you asked and things I never agreed to. Pay me my money, and let me go," said Thomas.

41

Kelly clenched her jaw and closed her eyes.

"Willie, take Thomas downstairs to our hideaway. Give him what he wants."

"But I thought …"

"Just do it," Eric interrupted. The brief conversation was followed by heavy breathing and a momentary stillness.

Stairs creaked in her direction, and she didn't dare move. The door swung open, flooding the room with light. Kelly held her breath and strained to ignore the pins and needles. Her foot screamed at her until she couldn't tolerate the sensation any longer, and she stretched her leg. The Bible hit the ground with a loud thump. She quickly stuffed the book back into her pocket and froze.

"There you are." Eric shoved the chest of drawers aside and grabbed Kelly, forcing her arms behind her back.

"You're hurting me!" she cried, attempting to wriggle free.

The gag made it difficult to breathe, and the yellow rope dug into her wrists. She struggled to hang on to the rickety railing, relying on her gymnastic training for balance. Eric's lantern flickered as he dragged her past the first floor and descended an endless flight of stairs. But Kelly stayed on her feet, estimating the distance between each tread until she reached the bottom step. The lantern dimmed to a soft glow and then went dark. Eric's hands pinched her shoulders, pushing her to the dirt. Footsteps and a bobbing light approached from the tunnel.

"What took so long? Did you settle with Thomas?" Eric asked, reaching into his jacket.

"Yeh, I took care of him. What do we do with her?" Willie shined the beam of his flashlight into Kelly's face, making her eyes water.

"Leave her in the storage room. No one will think to look for her there." Eric gripped her elbow and handed Willie the key. Kelly's heart beat faster as Willie turned the brass skeleton key and dragged her inside. Eric forced her to sit in a captain's chair and tied the ropes so tight dug into her ankles. "Grab the flashlight, and let's get out of here."

"This place gives me the creeps," said Willie, racing out of the room. The heavy door slammed shut. Kelly heard the key turn the lock, sealing her fate.

"Wait, I dropped the key! It sunk into the mud," said Willie.

"You idiot. Forget it. We'll never find it, and neither will she."

Eric's and Willie's voices grew distant. Alone, nobody to rescue her—not even her father—no one who knew the danger she faced or where to find her. The darkness closed around her as a sickening sound made her skin crawl. Soft moans turned into a blood-curdling scream. Recognizing the voice, Kelly squirmed and tore at her ropes.

"Ambrose! Oh, no, I will not be stuck here with you!"

She doubled over in her lap to pull the pocketknife from her sock and used her teeth to release the blade. The awkward position between her hands made it difficult to cut the rope, but sheer terror gave her the strength. She stuffed the knife into her front pocket, leaped from the chair, and collided into an old trunk. Her flashlight app lit the path to the door through a maze of antique desks, chairs, bedsprings, and dressers. The door was locked tight. Kelly pounded the heavy frame until her knuckles bled. She sank to her knees and aimed the light from her phone under the gap beneath the door. There had to be a way to find the key. She stood and rummaged through drawers, looking for any object to help her fish for the key.

Something crunched under her foot. Ambrose's bones lay in the corner in his tattered, bloodstained uniform. Louis Thompson left his body in an abandoned room, rotting for over a century! The horror of his death made her more determined than ever to leave Ambrose's bones behind. A candlestick missed her by inches, followed by repeated crashes in the dark. Kelly's jaw dropped as the angry spirit lifted a workbench in the air just as a white orb floated between her and Ambrose. Josephine's translucent body materialized, sending sparks in all directions, and smashed the bench against the wall.

Kelly scrambled past a clothes rack reeking of mothballs and bumped into a row of empty hangers. She grabbed a hanger and followed Josephine to the exit. Sore from being forced on the ground, she ignored the pain and fell to her knees, casting the metal wire through the gap beneath the door. The brass key, half covered in muck, caught on the hanger. She dragged the key under the door. After wiping the mud on her jeans, Kelly twisted the key into the lock. She unlocked the door and bolted into the dark, slamming the door behind her. A faint glow from her phone showed the staircase to the right and the entrance to a tunnel. She walked straight ahead, praying she picked the right passageway to find her family.

Kelly heard a muffled cry reverberate off the bricks. Shaking, she touched the walls, edging closer to the sound, trying not to react to odd clumps of slime and moss. Tunnels veered off in several directions, and if she picked the wrong one, it might lead her straight to the madmen who tried to kill her. Then her phone went dark. Frozen in her tracks, her chest tightened, forcing her to take shallow breaths.

Louis Thompson had thrown Ambrose's bloody corpse into the storeroom and left him to rot. Kelly remembered Lincoln's words: "A house divided against itself cannot stand." Ambrose paid the ultimate price. Hadn't she contributed to her own home being split in two, always fighting with her mom? *What if "I hate you" are the last words she hears from me?* Kelly wondered.

"I won't let it end this way!" Her scream echoed through the dark tunnel and bounced back. She wiped sweat from her cheek and continued stumbling on stray stones and wading through deep puddles. A faint light emanated ahead. She strained to hear familiar sounds, but there was only an eerie silence disturbed by occasional drips. A sick feeling swept over her as the door burst open and Eric and Willie waiting for her.

CHAPTER 8

────────◆────────

LINCOLN'S BUNKER

"**Y**ou're kidding me," said Eric, grabbing her arm and flinging her on the couch beside Thomas, who crumpled in a heap.

"What did you do to him?" She glared at her captor and put her arm around Thomas's hunched shoulders.

"Thanks to Thomas, we tracked you. He gave us blueprints to the tunnels and the underground bunker. But now, his services are no longer needed."

"You thank him by beating him?" Kelly asked, unable to shake her feelings of both outrage and affection toward Thomas.

Eric tied her hands and feet and tightened the ropes holding Thomas. "Don't worry. You'll both be dead soon. And this time for real!" His stare sent a shiver through Kelly, setting off dark and frightening images of the future.

"Do we have to kill them?" Willie asked.

"We don't want any witnesses. I've watched over you ever since we lost Mom and Dad in the car accident. I'm doing this for both of us. Shut up, and help me search. The gold has to be here," Eric told his brother.

"We've searched this entire place. Where else could it be?" asked Willie, following Eric to the kitchen, stepping on a squeaky floorboard.

Kelly heard them talking about a letter they found in the attic from their great-grandmother, Kate Warne, a spy working with the Allan Pinkerton Detective Agency. Kelly listened and learned Confederate gold coins mysteriously disappeared from an overturned wagon. Allan told

Kate that he hid the gold in an old copper mine underneath Wildwood Plantation to support Lincoln and the Union army.

Eric stepped into an adjacent room while Willie disappeared down a lengthy corridor, leaving Thomas and Kelly alone. She stared at the ebony and marble chess set on the table. Thomas grumbled and struggled to sit upright on the green-striped sofa. "What happened?"

"We're in trouble. I am so angry with you, I can't breathe."

"I'm sorry. I hadn't counted on feeling this way about you. But when they tried to kill us in the cabin, I tried to protect you. You ignored my warnings and insisted we go back into the mansion," replied Thomas, staring at his feet.

"Why did you agree to work with them in the first place?"

"Like I told you, my parents got this great idea to buy a farm in Virginia. All my friends are back in Washington DC. In six months, I'll be eighteen and independent. Eric offered me a ton of money if I agreed to help them. When I learned my mistake, I was in too deep."

The sound of tossed drawers and chairs exploded in a thunderous fury, startling Kelly. Eric returned moments later to stack his plunder next to the doorway.

Willie reappeared, rattling a lumpy canvas bag. "I found Mary Todd Lincoln's jewelry!"

"Great, search the galley for silver," Eric said over his shoulder and disappeared into Lincoln's bedroom.

Kelly wiggled her wrists to loosen the yellow clothesline and seized the moment alone. "How can I trust you?"

"Haven't you ever done something you regret and wish you could take back?" Thomas's blue eyes penetrated her heart, making her feel sorry for him.

"I have to rescue Grandpa and Brandan. Do you know where they are? Have you known this entire time?"

"Yes, but I realized how much I cared about you and tried to stay one step ahead of them. Eric and Willie cornered me when you located the second-floor secret passageway. Eric threatened to kill me and your family if I refused to cooperate. He wasn't bluffing."

Kelly's eyes narrowed, trying to wrap her head around the fact that he knew where they were being held captive this whole time.

"When I read the letter from Abe's hat, they were waiting for you nearby?" asked Kelly.

Thomas turned his head and kicked a box under the table.

"Brilliant plan 'cause now they are going to succeed," said Kelly.

"I didn't mean for anyone to get hurt. I tried to outsmart them, but they caught on."

Kelly sighed deeply. Willie reappeared and dropped his knapsack with a thud near the exit. He picked up an empty pillowcase and stomped past Kelly, his heavy boots creaking on the brittle floorboards.

"Did you hear that?" asked Eric, reappearing from Lincoln's bedroom.

"What?" Willie asked as he opened the pillowcase to stuff in two candlesticks.

"Step on that board again," said Eric.

"Ow," Willie said, stomping until the slat broke.

Eric drew a hunting knife from his pocket. He glanced in Kelly's direction with a malicious grin as the floorboard shattered into brittle pieces.

"They raised the floorboards to protect it from dampness. The gold has to be underneath. Fetch the crowbar, and help me flip the bed in Lincoln's bedroom," said Eric.

Willie followed orders without question.

A loud crash shook the rug underneath her toes and rattled a door behind the love seat. The battery-operated hurricane lamp left by Eric cast eerie shadows. She noticed a door behind the couch and wondered if it led to an exit. The sound of sliding furniture made Kelly's stomach turn, realizing they didn't have long before that maniac fulfilled his promise.

"We found two bags of gold," Eric shouted, running into the room with a bulging canvas bag. He raced toward the couch and slid a cardboard box from underneath the table, shoving the chess set to the floor.

Kelly's jaw dropped at the sight of the homemade bomb made with TNT and electronics.

"Don't you love the dark internet?" asked Eric.

"The timer is automatically set at twenty minutes, giving you a little more time to live. The lamp is fading, but you'll still see the countdown until the explosion." Eric activated the device.

"I left a light burning in Mary Todd Lincoln's room," Willie said as he tossed a water bottle, hitting Thomas in the head. Thomas wailed and fell to his side. Blood dripped from his forehead.

"Do we really have to kill them, Eric?"

"Shut up and run!"

CHAPTER 9

EXPLOSION

Eric and Willie's footsteps faded, and the timer ticked closer to detonation. Kelly remembered Brandan's knife in the bottom of her pocket. She used two fingers to yank it free. She released the blade with her teeth, ignoring the twang as it opened. The yellow rope was frayed and loosened, allowing her to cut the ropes from her ankles and then free Thomas.

"Where did they go?" asked Thomas, grumbling and rubbing his wrists. The color drained from his cheeks.

"You fainted. Eric and Willie are gone. We're running out of time! Can you stand?"

"I think can. I'm so sorry I lied to you." He wobbled and grabbed the armrest for balance.

"Save your apologies for later. We have to act fast. Do you know how to defuse a homemade bomb?"

Thomas stared at the device. "The corroded TNT is unstable, and they rigged detonators to explode if anyone messes with the wires."

Kelly dashed to the mysterious door behind the couch and turned the knob. The door lurched open, revealing a machine labeled "oxygen control." Pipes crisscrossed above made hissing noises. She returned to pick up the box with the bomb; but Thomas placed his hand on her wrist.

"Wait. I got us into this, let me risk my life," said Thomas. His watery eyes begged her to forgive him. He staggered and fell onto the couch.

"You're too unsteady," Kelly said, aware he was more injured than he admitted, and their chances of survival would remain slim if left to him.

Thomas sighed, nodded, and waited on the sofa. Kelly held her breath, lifted the cardboard box containing the explosive materials, and imagined herself floating through space as she had done countless times in her gymnastic routine. What seemed like an eternity lapsed before she reached the far end of the ventilation room. Her hands wavered and challenged her nerves as she set the explosive device on the cement. Lights started blinking on the apparatus, and she raced through the exit, closing the door behind her.

Thomas grabbed her hand to stand. She wrapped her arm around his waist and moved as fast as possible, his arm growing heavy around her shoulder. Heart racing, she dragged him into the Mary Todd Lincoln bedroom and let him slump to the floor against the far corner. With just moments to spare, she closed the door and pressed a chest of drawers tight against the entryway, hoping to contain the damage.

"Help me move this mattress," said Kelly. Silence met her request, and she knew he had passed out. Kelly's muscles strained and yanked the yellowed, foul-smelling mattress over their heads. She braced herself and prayed for a miracle.

Seconds later, the explosion rocked the shelter. Kelly felt the intense pressure on her chest, pushing her hard against the wall. The quilted mattress landed on her feet, while Thomas lay still.

"Thomas!" She shook him. "Wake up!" The prospect of dying alone crushed under tons of rock, without a single person aware of her location, made her cringe. She trembled, wondering if her brother and grandfather survived the explosion. Tears cascaded and turned into sobs.

"Take it easy, will you?" Thomas opened his eyelids, choking on a violent cough as blood sprayed into his palm. She wrapped her arms around him and didn't want to let go.

"Quit scaring me. You need a hospital, and I'm going to see if there's another way out." Kelly grabbed the lantern.

"Please hurry. I'm not feeling well."

Kelly pushed the bureau aside, banging it into an umbrella stand. She stepped back and jumped across a wide crevice, landing on solid ground. Kelly raced through the hallway to find Lincoln's bedroom blocked by timber and rubble. The demolished door to the tunnel, living room, and ventilation chamber shattered her hopes of finding a way out. Bricks, rocks, and dirt covered the sofa, where they'd been sitting moments before. More fallout could happen at any time. Then a glint from the debris caught her eye as she adjusted to the fading light. She swung the lantern closer and found gold coins scattered among the shadows. Kelly shrieked. A severed hand still clutched a torn canvas bag.

CHAPTER 10

BURIED ALIVE

Eric died, his blood spattered across the wreckage. How long before evil penetrated Wildwood Plantation, haunted by his corpse? Efforts to rescue Kelly's grandfather and brother failed. Should she tell Thomas the fate of the madman? She squinted as the lamp dimmed into a faint glow, and she noticed the dark hole in front of Mary Todd Lincoln's room too late. Panic raced through her as she slipped and caught herself inching backwards until she reached safety. She moved to her mark, took a running jump, and landed next to the dresser.

"You okay? I heard you scream," said Thomas.

"The bomb wrecked everything on the far side of the bunker, including the ventilation system."

"You're kidding me! You're telling me we're trapped?" Thomas attempted to rise, wavered, and collapsed to the floor.

"Eric's dead. I discovered his body in the rubble," said Kelly, recalling the image of his dismembered hand. Thomas deserved to know the truth.

"How did he die?" asked Thomas, his voice clearly agitated.

"We heard them leave, but he must have returned. Why did he do that? They forgot something?" asked Kelly.

"What a monster! He destroyed himself trying to kill us!" said Thomas, rolling on his side and screaming in agony.

"I think you have a broken rib," said Kelly. She dragged the mattress onto the bed frame. Wiping the sweat from her forehead, she helped Thomas to lie on the bed.

In her wildest imagination, she never imagined dying this way. Even if she escaped, how could she take Thomas in his condition? No matter what, she'd never abandon him. But the odds of finding a way out grew dimmer with the fading light.

The lantern died minutes later, and Kelly's hopes threatened to die with it. She turned from the bed and touched the nearest wall, hoping to find something to lead to an exit. The bureau had oriented her to the open doorway when a desperate and hopeless feeling took hold. What if the explosion buried her family in this rubble? What if she led Brandan to his death? How could she ever forgive herself?

Kelly squirmed on a hard chair near the bed, struggling for air. It had been hours since the explosion, and she had found nothing to help them escape.

"My head hurts. I feel woozy," said Thomas as he held out his hand for hers. His warmth flowed through her, and she returned his affection. But Kelly was not sure if she felt forgiveness or hopelessness.

"Did you hear that? Something's moving in my direction!" She jumped to her feet. Did Willie survive? She dismissed the idea and froze, not daring to breathe as a slimy creature slithered over her sneakers and wrapped around her ankles.

Fear crushed her ability to speak until she uttered a faint, "Copperhead!"

"This is unbelievable," said Thomas, moaning as bedsprings squeaked from across the room.

"Stay on the bed. My brother showed me what to do."

Kelly shoved the dresser aside, opened the exit, and gripped a cane from the umbrella stand. She struggled to peel the snake off her with the cane's curved handle. Pressure tightened against her shins. Anger welled inside her. Kelly knew she had to act fast before the snake bit her and released its poisonous venom. The squirming copperhead dangled on the cane as she tore the viper from her legs and flung it far into the open passageway. Her hands shook with terror. She threw the walking stick into the chasm and slammed the door shut.

"I refuse to die here," vowed Kelly, her heart racing. Kelly heard Thomas stumble to his feet and slump into the wobbly armchair.

"What's going to happen to us?" Thomas asked.

Kelly sighed. No one was going to rescue them. What if Lincoln's enemies trapped him in the bunker? Allan Pinkerton and Louis Thompson built so many intricate hiding places, they must have thought of an escape route for the president. She fought for deeper breaths and tried to ignore the heavy feeling in her chest, but the idea gave her hope.

"Lend me your phone," said Kelly, feeling a new surge of energy.

"I used it when you explored the other side of the bunker. I'm not sure how much power's left," Thomas said. She grabbed his cell and helped him to lean on her shoulder.

"Lincoln had an escape route. Otherwise, they'd trap themselves in the shelter. We need to find the secret door. Screen's dim, but the flashlight works," said Kelly, feeling light-headed.

Their last-ditch effort to break free of the tunnels weighed on her. She had to trust the builders of Lincoln's sanctuary to protect him from his enemies. She scrutinized picture frames, dressers, and bookcases, searching for a hidden mechanism. An hour later, her hopes faded with the battery.

"We're almost out of air," said Kelly. Her energy and enthusiasm waning, she sank to the ground. She took Thomas's hand to help him sit beside her.

"I am sorry I got you into this," he said.

Kelly inched away and closed her eyes, willing her second sight to show her a way to escape. The unmistakable aroma of lilacs compelled her to glance upward. A soft glow illuminated the image of a woman in a black, flowing dress motioning toward a tapestry. The uneven planks scraped Kelly's shins as she crawled across the floor and grabbed the corner of the tapestry. The large, dusty wall hanging dropped on top of her head, making her cough. She squirmed and tossed it off her shoulders. Tears welled and hope flooded over her as Josephine's aura of light shined on a door.

"You won't believe this!" She helped Thomas stand while he grumbled and moaned. Louis Thompson's wife glowed, her transparent figure close. Kelly tried to touch her, but her hand passed through her skirts into nothingness.

"Are we dead? Is that a door?" Thomas asked, his voice shaking.

"Stay with me," said Kelly, standing inches from the wooden panel. The brass knob turned halfway and stopped. "Unbelievable. It's locked! Where in the world is the key?" Kelly asked sinking to the floor. She doubted they had the strength to kick the door open. A sharp pain seared her chest, and movement proved difficult with the thinning oxygen. *Why didn't I find the way out earlier?*

The lady in black's spirit disappeared into the pitch-blackness. Kelly groped in the dark, disappointed that Josephine had abandoned her. Closing her eyes, she remembered the bunker blueprints and the letter to Louis Thompson tucked inside the Bible. The book in her back pocket had survived for over a century and provided historic clues leading to Lincoln's bunker. Touching the cover, she again noticed its lumpy spine, which had come slightly apart earlier. Kelly stuck her finger deep into the column. She felt a small metal object lodged at the base, and her heart beat faster as she shook it hard. A key fell into her lap. Kelly used her last ounce of strength to insert the key into the lock.

The hardwood door pushed open against years of neglect. Kelly dragged Thomas into the dank atmosphere. She tried to imagine herself free, but the tunnel seemed to endlessly stretch before them. And she was slowed by Thomas leaning heavily on her shoulders.

Eric's bloody body haunted her. She pushed onward, leading Thomas by the hand. Lincoln's bunker descended four flights to the former mine entrance. The arduous trek through a maze of tunnels made it impossible to gauge their progress. The air grew lighter with each step as the surface loomed ahead.

"We'll never escape. It's a dead end, and my head hurts," said Thomas, splashing puddles of mud in every direction.

"Stop whining. Secret doors have what in common?" asked Kelly.

"I don't know. I'm too tired to guess, unless you mean a lever."

"Help me find it!" Kelly yelled, feeling her blood pressure rising.

"You want me to touch slimy walls with snakes and bats hiding in the corners? Are you crazy?" Thomas squirmed and pulled away.

Panic threatened to derail her, but Kelly knew she needed his help. A breeze blew across her cheek as if somebody shook her awake. The draft poured through a crack at the end of the tunnel. She patted the bricks and slid her fingers over disgusting craters. A sticky substance clung to her palm. She slapped aside something crawling up her arm and discovered a nest of spiders and cobwebs.

"Okay, I'll help," Thomas sighed.

Together they scraped away the cobwebs until a gray veil of light bordered the exit and exposed the lever. She kicked the pedal, producing a grinding noise, and pushed hard against the heavy metal door, fighting the weeds. The door opened partway. Fragrant air filled her lungs and her courage as she and Thomas bounded into the woods.

"We made it!" said Thomas. "I can't believe it," he said, hugging her.

She welcomed his warmth and felt relief in his arms. But when he leaned in for a kiss, she withdrew. She wanted no more tricks. He shrugged and collapsed on a granite rock.

"My ribs are killing me. Where are we?" he asked, looking rejected.

Challenged to figure out the best route, she scanned the horizon for the best options. "This doorway exits a mile beyond the tunnels and the mansion, but in what direction? The Blue Ridge Mountains lie behind the tree line. We need to go left of the mine entrance," Kelly said with confidence, masking the fact that she was guessing.

"Take me to my family, please," Kelly said, desperate to learn what happened to them.

"I'll take you, but I'm not sure what we will find."

They waded through ferns encircling a towering pine tree. The fresh air and earthy scent revived her. Thomas struggled, but she had no sympathy. Deep shadows settled, casting a murky light and making it harder to distinguish the forest from the mountains. A gunshot echoed in the distance.

"Listen." Thomas turned to face Kelly and clenched his fist. "Willie's alive?"

Kelly crept behind a fir tree, pulling Thomas beside her. She peeked at Willie slumped next to a bag of stolen treasure.

"This is my fault. If I hadn't forgotten the second bag of gold in Lincoln's bedroom, you'd still be alive. You promised you'd never leave me. What am I supposed to do now?" asked Willie, waving his gun and blubbering.

"What a rat," said Thomas under his breath.

Kelly stepped aside to let him see for himself, but he grew careless and stepped on a fallen branch, snapping it in two. Willie turned to face the fir tree. His red, swollen eyes glared above the barrel of his gun.

CHAPTER 11

REVENGE

"**M**y brother's dead because of you!" He fired at Kelly's foot. A second round blasted off a branch that landed on Thomas's head. She gripped his hand and fled, dodging Willie's bullets.

"I hate that guy," said Thomas, clutching his rib, reminding Kelly he needed a doctor.

"How could brothers be so different? We're lucky it wasn't Eric," she said. Eric tried to bury her under the rubble and might have succeeded if she hadn't remembered Brandan's knife. The mansion appeared in the distance, and she prayed her family survived.

The immense double doors swung into the ballroom. She hurried into the parlor while Thomas yanked the lever at the base of the fireplace. The secret passage lurched into the stilted air that challenged her senses as they made their way along the narrow hallway. He stopped and held the tapestry for her to duck under. She remembered walking past the wall hanging and realized it hung next to the room with the dumbwaiter. She descended two flights of stairs to a landing and heard voices.

"They'd better be okay," said Kelly. She nudged Thomas aside and burst into a cramped space with a soiled mattress, an empty dumbwaiter, and no windows.

"What took you so long?" Brandan asked, hugging his sister, who also received an unexpected hug from the caretaker. Relief flooded over her seeing everyone alive.

The caretaker tore off the other sleeve of his jersey and replaced the bandage around Grandpa's head.

"Is everyone okay?" asked Kelly.

"Grandpa got the worst of it when Eric clobbered him and transported him here, but then an explosion shook plaster on our heads."

She grasped her grandfather's hand and felt his warmth as he opened his eyes.

"The medication you dropped in the shaft saved him, but he is losing too much blood," said Brandan, helping her lift him to his feet.

"How could you do this?" Kelly whispered to Thomas in the passageway as they neared the fireplace exit. "You made me search everywhere when you knew where they were." She squeezed her fingers into a fist, outraged at his betrayal.

The hearth opened, making her aware of her hatred of closed spaces. Police sirens broke the silence. Eerie shadows and ghosts from the Civil War followed her past the piano in the main hall through the towering columns to the crumbling steps outside. Two law enforcement cars screeched to a halt, scraping the stone lion and flooding Kelly with hope. The police signaled the end of this nightmare.

"Everyone okay?" asked the sheriff as he reached for the walkie-talkie to call the station.

"They injured my grandfather, and with his heart condition, he needs a hospital. Thomas might have a concussion and several broken ribs," answered Kelly as she lowered Thomas on the bottom porch step. She relayed the events and mentioned that Eric died in the blast, and his younger brother, Willie, survived. "You need to find him. He's armed and unstable."

Sheriff Martin sent his deputy to search for Willie. "I've phoned for an ambulance. It should be here soon," said the sheriff.

The caretaker aided Grandpa into the backseat of the squad car. Numbness spread over her as she slumped next to Brandan on the steps. Did any of this happen? A bulge underneath her right side made it uncomfortable to sit. She stood and pulled the small Bible with historic clues from Abraham Lincoln, Allan Pinkerton, and Louis Thompson from her pocket. The book—and Josephine, her guardian angel—saved her life.

"My deputy informs me there's no sign of the younger brother. We found Jeremiah and the kids, but we're still looking for Jeremiah's son-in-law," The sheriff reported over the radio to the station.

"Edward, my dad? He's here?" Kelly asked, searching in all directions. She wished she could summon her second sight to find her father.

Willie, with glaring red eyes, jumped from behind the azalea bush and aimed his weapon at Thomas before the sheriff could answer. Brandan grabbed her arm and dragged her behind the lion statue. She lay on her stomach, praying, too frightened to move.

"Willie, give me the pistol. You're not a murderer," said a familiar voice. "Dad?"

Her brother nodded, affirming their father's identity, when a bullet rang out, followed by a blood-curdling scream.

"Son, listen to the man. I don't want to hurt you," said the sheriff.

She peeked over the lion's mane just as Willie spun to target the sheriff. The lawman drew a revolver from his holster. Another blast ripped into the atmosphere, and Willie sank to the ground. Sheriff Martin kneeled to take his pulse.

"I'm afraid he's dead." The sheriff secured the gun and reported the incident to headquarters. "Poor kid. I wonder if he realized he'd run out of bullets."

Kelly felt sorry for Willie. He never wanted to hurt anyone.

Thomas remained still under the flowering azalea bush. Kelly shrieked at the sight of his shirt soaked with blood. She stood to find Henry, the caretaker, kneeling at his side. The old man threw his wig on the ground, tore off his mask, and put pressure on Thomas's shoulder to stop the bleeding. His jet-black hair hovered over Thomas as tufts of beard and spirit gum clung to his face.

"Dad, you're the caretaker?" asked Kelly.

Her father glanced upward, confirming his identity. Shock jolted her as she remembered Grandpa's missing makeup kit. Thanks to Grandpa's skill and artistry, she never recognized her father. The genuine concern she felt from him as they searched the estate made sense now, and she found it hard to contain her excitement.

"We have things to discuss, but they have to wait. Hope you never forgot how much I love you," said Kelly's dad.

The EMS transport backed into the driveway near the sheriff's vehicle.

Her dad helped the paramedics load the stretcher and stayed with her grandfather. The paramedic wrapped Thomas's shoulder, and Kelly watched the ambulance drive away with the three of them.

The back seat of the police car smelled of old sandwiches, while empty cans of soda clinked at her feet. Kelly sat next to her brother listening to the chatter on the police scanner. Sheriff Martin left his deputies to secure the scene and sped through traffic to the nearest hospital in Leesville, Virginia.

"I got a message from your mom. She'll meet you both in the emergency room," said Sheriff Martin.

Kelly froze with dread at the thought of facing her mother.

The sirens startled Kelly, adding to the sick feeling in her stomach as the sheriff pulled into the emergency wing of the hospital. Medical center policy mandated she be transported in a wheelchair. She hung on tight while a nurse wheeled her into the emergency room at breakneck speed. Curtains surrounded the lumpy mattress, and the closed-in cubicle made her want to scream. She needed to get out of there and find out what happened to Grandpa and Thomas.

Adrenaline raced through her veins as the icy flooring sent shivers through her bare feet. The trip past thirty separate cubicles in the trauma center led to a glass entryway. Dread and hope mingled, but just as she pushed the metal bar to join her mother in the waiting room, a hand caught her elbow.

"Excuse me, miss. Please return to the cubicle. I need to finish your exam," said a nurse in white with a stethoscope hanging around her neck. The chill caused her to tiptoe with caution past the long line of curtains before she recognized her sneakers. The minute the nurse left her alone, she dove into her shoes without bothering to lace them. She raced past the long line of curtains and pushed the cold metal bar into the waiting room.

A woman in her early forties sat hunched, protecting her face with her hands. "Mom?"

"Kelly? Oh my God, are you okay?"

"What's wrong? Is it Grandpa?" asked Kelly, holding her breath.

"They wheeled him into surgery. The doctors are checking on his triple bypass to look for internal bleeding. But because of his skull injury and loss of blood, they question his chance of survival," her mother explained.

Kelly's eyes watered, but no tears appeared. She'd give everything to spare her mother more drama, but an opportunity presented itself to clear the air.

"I'm so sorry I acted the way I did when you broke the news of the divorce. It shocked and horrified me. But after everything that's happened, I've learned our family will be there for each other."

"I'm glad you know that now. I will always love you," said her mom. She welcomed her mother's embrace, holding her close.

"Young lady, I will not ask you again. We're too busy to chase you," the nurse said, grabbing Kelly's arm and escorting her back to the lumpy mattress. Poked and prodded, she squirmed through the tests and stared at the ceiling until a medical assistant returned with the results.

"You're dehydrated. If you drink a bottle of water every half hour, you can wait with your parents," said the nurse, removing the wires from her arm and turning off the monitor.

The water reminded her of the first breaths of fresh air when she and Thomas emerged from the tunnel. Brandan appeared from an adjacent curtain, and they joined their parents on a blue couch.

"Dad, why did you wait so long to let us know it was you?" asked Brandan.

"Grandpa created my disguise as a caretaker to avoid suspicion after we uncovered the discovery of a lifetime. We spent days studying Louis Thompson's journals, history books, and antique letters for clues to the underground tunnels and Lincoln's bunker. The guy covered in tattoos grabbed Jeremiah as he photographed the gravestones in the cemetery. I had to hide my identity and the fact that I work for the government," he answered.

"Kelly, why is your face more twisted than normal?" asked Brandan.

She glanced away from his intense stare. "Eric is dead, buried with Confederate gold coins in Lincoln's bunker. I know I'm safe now, but the image of his bloody severed hand haunts me."

"Edward, I swear, you and my papa. You kids had no business prowling in that dilapidated mansion," said their mom, scowling and throwing her hands in the air.

The doctor appeared in blue scrubs to talk to their parents. Kelly inched closer to listen to what he had to say. "Luckily for Jeremiah, your children were there. The kids delivered his medication and found him before he experienced a fatal heart attack. He's going to recover."

Kelly welcomed her mother's arms; joined by her dad and Brandan. Elated everyone was safe, she inhaled deeply ready to accept whatever the future held for her family.

She filled them in on the terrifying events, unable to believe them herself. "Eric smashed an old lodge to smithereens, and we escaped with seconds to spare. Later, he locked me in an abandoned storage closet with Ambrose's bones."

"How did the kid from the general store get involved? And who in the world is Ambrose?" Brandan grilled her with questions until their father raised his palm to stop the interrogation. Kelly smiled and clasped his arm, grateful to be let off the hook.

"And what happened to my Boy Scout knife?" Brandan asked.

Kelly reached into her sock and handed him the knife that had saved her life more than once. She excused herself and raced to find a restroom. Her heart refused to listen to the warnings in her head. She needed to find Thomas and noticed a deputy sitting next to an open door.

"I want to check on my friend," said Kelly.

"Not sure he's your friend, but you may have a brief visit," said the guard. The officer surveyed the room before allowing her to enter.

Kelly tiptoed in, unsure of the reception waiting for her.

"Go away," Thomas said, closing his eyes.

"Tell me what the doctor said. Please!" Kelly walked to the other side of the bed and waited until he glanced at her.

"I have three cracked ribs, a concussion, and a bullet wound in my shoulder. That should make you happy since you despise me so much."

"I don't despise you."

"Why do you care? Why did you save my life multiple times?"

"I've been asking myself that same thing. When you have feelings for a person, those feelings don't disappear because you tell them to," said Kelly, feeling light-headed.

"I have the same problem. I think I'm falling in love with you, especially after you saved my life. You might as well know they're charging me with aiding and abetting the kidnappers. My parents hired a lawyer, and he says they might make allowances for extenuating circumstances and reduce the sentence to community service. Everything I did was to protect you from Eric and Willie, especially after they tried to kill us in the shack. They never lost sight of our movements or let an opportunity slip past to corner me."

Thomas grasped her hand in his. His blue eyes sent a shiver down to her toes. "My God, your hands are like ice."

The room spun. Kelly grabbed for the railing, but her grip slipped. She blacked out just as her head hit the floor.

CHAPTER 12

WILDWOOD PLANTATION

Kelly opened her eyes to a familiar beeping sound and an IV protruding from her right arm. "Welcome back. Your dehydrated condition reached a dangerous level, and since you won't listen, I have an alternative method of replacing the liquid you've lost," said a familiar nurse, checking her pulse and taking her blood pressure.

"I'll follow directions. Please let me go," said Kelly.

"Prove yourself after we've stabilized you. In the meantime, relax. Your family can come to you." Soon after the nurse left, Kelly found her bed surrounded.

"We have good news," said her mother. "Your father and I plan to try to work things out and not get a divorce."

"Cleaning out and rescuing artifacts from Lincoln's bunker will take time, so we are moving into Grandpa's house. The government needs to search for a new agent. Nothing is more important than my family," said her dad as he squeezed her free hand.

Tears that dehydration prevented earlier flowed. Kelly wiped them with the sleeve of her dressing gown.

"But Grandpa's home is a refrigerator," said Brandan, shaking his head.

"We are moving to Virginia, and we'll find a place of our own. I promise," said their dad. Brandan threw himself into his father's arms. Kelly couldn't wait to do that herself.

The next day, Kelly dressed and raced down the aisle of the emergency room to check on Thomas. Cries of pain rose from behind the emergency room curtains, making her realize others suffered with worse injuries. She retraced her steps, recognizing the double doors that led to the trauma center and the room beyond. The guard no longer sat in his chair. Kelly walked in to find a freshly made bed and wondered if she had the right room. Her foot hit a gold coin that must have fallen out of her pocket when she fell the day before, but there was no sign of Thomas.

Six Months Later

Kelly pulled her bicycle to the side of the road to secure the blossoms in her basket and check the map for the turnoff to Wildwood Plantation. A car loaded with groceries sped by, forcing her close to the edge of a ditch.

She loved their modern house with lots of windows, comfortable furniture, and no ghosts. Her parents, busy setting up her father's office in the basement, didn't notice her slip out the door. Her heart ached, wondering what happened to Thomas. He just vanished from the hospital.

She turned a mile beyond the fire station, relieved the paved route was easier than the bike path. The estate emerged through the row of oak trees. She parked her bike at the bottom of the hill below the cemetery. She had no intention of going inside Wildwood Plantation. But the faded white pillars compelled her to face them. The intense rush of adrenaline warned her as a shadow crossed the second-floor alcove window. She gritted her teeth and shook it off.

Kelly gathered her flowers and climbed to the spiked iron fence. The mowed lawn bore no resemblance to the earlier time, when weeds surrounded the stones. Josephine's polished monument rose in place of the broken headstone, courtesy of the government. Kelly arranged flowers on her grave as a faint translucent figure in a black flowing skirt materialized in front of her.

"My dad discovered this letter in Ambrose's uniform when he sent his bones to his ancestors in South Carolina. I want to read it to you," Kelly said to the apparition. She withdrew a copy of the yellowed note from her shirt pocket.

Dear Penelope, news has reached me that we are expecting a blessed event. I miss you and wish I had never left. Lee tells us we can win, but at what cost? I've been captured and stuck in a terrible Yankee prisoner of war camp in Washington DC. Hunger, disease, and death surround me. I plan to escape Old Brick Capitol Prison tonight. I have to take the chance. I'm coming home to you and our child. If God sees fit to take my soul, pray for me. Forever yours, A.

"My dad discovered that Penelope and his son did not survive the birth. Ambrose's spirit is free and buried beside his wife and unborn infant. I hope you find peace. I'll never be able to repay you," said Kelly.

A soft, glowing light grew brighter, rose above the apparition, and faded into the horizon.

"Incredible!" A dark-haired boy with penetrating blue eyes stared at her through the fence.

She jumped to her feet as leaves and baby's breath rolled from her lap. Thomas stood in the narrow opening of the heavy gate.

"I spotted you on my way to deliver groceries to the food shelf. Your grandfather banned me from the museum, but I had to see you," he said, walking toward her.

Kelly's hands trembled as her emotions flew in every direction after spending weeks letting go of the horror and betrayal, and attempting to put everything in the past, including Thomas. "I went to find you in the hospital, but you were gone."

"My mom's a nurse, and they whisked me back to the hospital she used to work at in Washington DC. We returned to the farmhouse after my wounds heeled. The judge suspended the kidnapping charges and gave me a year of volunteering at the Leesville Village Center. It feels good to help people."

Kelly kneeled to rearrange the blooms on Josephine's gravestone. A hand touched her shoulder, and Thomas lifted her into his arms. He pressed his lips against hers, flooding her with warmth. She couldn't deny her heart any longer.

AUTHOR'S NOTES

I have a strong interest in history, especially Lincoln and the Civil War. I researched Allan Pinkerton's Detective Agency and learned how he spied for the Union and saved Lincoln's life while he rode a train to the capital. Allan Pinkerton enlisted women to spy in the South. He found places for President Lincoln to take refuge when he needed to get away, inspiring the Lincoln bunker underneath Wildwood Plantation. I also learned the Confederates turned their bank notes into gold coins and bars. During the Civil War, one of the shipments of gold traveling on a covered wagon disappeared. Allan Pinkerton may have stolen a partial shipment for the Union. People are still searching for the Confederate gold that was distributed and hidden across the country.

The following personal experience fueled an element of my story and is one I'll never forget. A conference held in Vermont took place at a renovated hotel previously abandoned and condemned for over thirty years. This hotel had been popular from 1769 through the 1950s and included guests such as Mary Todd Lincoln, American presidents Ulysses S. Grant, Benjamin Harrison, William Howard Taft, and Theodore Roosevelt. You can imagine the centuries of ghosts still wandering through those halls.

I was struggling with my magnetic key card to open my room on the third floor when I felt a presence standing directly behind me. I turned slowly, holding my breath, to see an odd-shaped door and sensed somebody close. Hairs stood up on the back of my neck as panic coursed through every fiber of my being. I ran toward the staircase and made it halfway to the top of the stairs when a rush of ice-cold electricity passed through my body, not once, but twice. Two entities raced down the stairwell and disappeared. Scared out of my mind, I kept this experience to myself, not wanting it to be real.

After dinner that evening, the manager talked about two kids who explored the condemned building and fell through rotten floorboards from the third floor and died. He told us that you can still hear them running up and down the hallway. I shared my story and found out many people, staff and guests heard them too.

I want to reinforce the importance of leaving your imagination to books and movies and to avoid condemned and abandoned buildings.

Printed in the United States
by Baker & Taylor Publisher Services